Bolan was halfway off the chair when the window exploded

As two men burst through the door, M-16s blazing, the Executioner squeezed off two rounds, dropping both gunners. Even as Bolan fired, he heard commotion behind him. He rolled onto his back, the Desert Eagle booming again as another hitter leaped through the broken glass of the window, a Colt Python filling his hand.

The first Magnum round drilled the man through the shoulder, blowing him back against the bar before a second round punched him to the floor.

Bolan jumped to his feet as two more Peruvian gunners entered the bar from the highway side. He whirled, finger already tightening on the trigger as a long burst of gunfire sailed harmlessly past his shoulder.

Suddenly all was quiet.

The Executioner barely had time to draw a breath before the second wave of the cartel's attack began....

MACK BOLAN.

The Executioner

DON PENDLETON'S®

THE EXECUTIONER

FEATURING MACK BOLAN®

CAYMAN STRIKE

A GOLD EAGLE BOOK FROM

WORLDWIDE.

TORONTO · NEW YORK · LONDON · PARIS
AMSTERDAM · STOCKHOLM · HAMBURG
ATHENS · MILAN · TOKYO · SYDNEY

First edition January 1992

ISBN 0-373-61157-9

Special thanks and acknowledgment to
Jerry VanCook for his contribution to this work.

CAYMAN STRIKE

Without justice, courage is weak.

—Benjamin Franklin

In the face of adversity it takes a strong man to see
justice done. It's easier to turn your back and
walk away.

—Mack Bolan

To the dedicated efforts of
the men and women of the DEA

PROLOGUE

Beads of sweat, salty and smelling faintly of ammonia, rolled down Reuben Gonzalez's neck to soak his shirt collar. He leaned back against the seat and closed his eyes. The dreary plop of the propeller relaxed the DEA special agent, slowly driving the demons from his soul. He opened his eyes. Through the window of the Beechcraft Baron, he saw the enormous continent of land behind them fade to a tiny speck on the horizon. Breathing a sigh of relief, Gonzalez leaned back again, loosened his seat belt and turned to his wife.

Tana stared stiffly ahead at the back of the pilot's neck, her face a mask of fear.

Gonzalez leaned forward, tapping the pilot on the shoulder. "Hey, Wally?"

Wally Webber twisted behind the controls, his huge white teeth flashing a grin as his eyebrows rose. "Yeah, Cha-cha?"

"How much farther?"

Webber shrugged, his huge shoulders bobbing quickly up and down. "Depends. We can fly straight on to D.C. if you want. But we might better change course—not take chances. What do *you* think?"

Gonzalez glanced toward Jim Rainey in the seat next to the pilot. Like Webber, Rainey wore a navy blue nylon "raid jacket" with the letters *DEA* emblazoned across the back. Almost as big as Webber, Rainey had a shock of chalk white hair and almost albino skin.

Gonzalez felt a chill rush over him. He was the ranking agent. It was his decision.

Webber broke into his thoughts. "Think about it," he said, and turned back to face the sky. "We've got a little time before we have to decide." He paused, and Gonzalez saw him take a deep breath. A worried look passed across his face and then, just as quickly, the look became an expression of indifference. "Those rumors are probably just that, Cha-cha. Rumors. I can't believe those maggots could get their hands on a plane like that. Or a gun." He paused again. "On the other hand, they've done some stuff that even the big boys in Medellín never pulled off. And I don't have to tell you, they damn sure don't want you testifying."

Gonzalez nodded. He crossed his arms and closed his eyes, leaning back in his seat again to concentrate on the sound of the propeller.

This time it didn't work.

The DEA agent took a deep breath. He was tired. He'd been undercover too long again, and that fine line between his adopted identity and who he really was had begun to fade. He opened his eyes and watched his wife out of the corner of his eye. Tana looked terrified, and that fried his brain even more.

No, Reuben Gonzalez told himself again, he wasn't in any shape emotionally to make decisions—particularly decisions that might make the difference between life and death. For all four of them.

Rainey pulled a crumpled pack of cigarettes from his shirt pocket and shook one to the top. His eyebrows rose slightly, and he turned and extended the pack over the seat toward Gonzalez.

The agent started to reach forward, then remembered that once again he'd promised Tana he'd quit smoking. Now didn't seem to be the ideal time for anything that might add to the stress, but he still couldn't bring himself to break his word. "No, thanks, Jim."

Suddenly the anger that sometimes came at the end of an undercover assignment replaced the DEA man's fatigue and fear. He felt the outrage rise from his chest to his throat. He wasn't just tired. He was sick and tired. Sick of the foolish, twisted feeling that somehow he was the criminal, he was the traitor.

Tired of the inevitable friendships he made undercover, regardless of how hard he tried not to.

He rested the palm of his hand on the grip of the SIG-Sauer 9 mm pistol in the holster at his side. The cool metal felt comforting under his fingers. He forced his mind back to the problem at hand.

He had to either decide to play it safe and take an alternate route, or decide that Wally was right; the Lima cartel boys couldn't possibly be equipped with a British air assault plane.

"Let's veer west, Wally," Gonzalez heard himself suddenly say. "You're probably right. Those guys did a lot of bragging. But there's no sense taking a chance." He felt his hands clench into tight, knotted fists. "If they're coming, they'll expect us to head straight toward Florida. We can refuel on Grand

Cayman, cut north over Mississippi or Alabama, then back east. Even those bastards won't come into American air space."

Without answering, Webber dipped the wing of the plane and they headed west.

Far below, Gonzalez watched the tiny waves as they danced across the ocean. He closed his eyes, and once again the propeller became an almost hypnotic force, driving the fear and anxiety from his heart. He glanced to his side. Even Tana appeared more relaxed. Maybe...

Webber's voice broke into his thoughts. "Shit," the pilot said.

He heard Rainey. "Huh?"

"Something coming up fast to the rear," Webber continued. "Same altitude. Oh...*shit.*"

Gonzalez felt the plane suddenly jerk. From somewhere behind came the distant sounds of automatic fire. They jerked again. He looked to Webber and saw sweat break out on the pilot's forehead. Through the window to his right, the DEA man saw smoke billowing around the wing.

Rainey turned toward Webber, his face a frightened mask of horror. "Wally..."

More gunfire, more jerking. Webber gripped the controls, the knuckles of his hands white.

The plane lurched again, and a shrill, whining squeal echoed through the cabin. Gonzalez's stomach jumped as they began to lose altitude. He opened his mouth to speak, but the words wouldn't come.

"Brace yourselves," Webber said, "we're going down." Below the calm, professional voice, Gonzalez could hear the terror.

He felt Tana's fingers lace through his and grip hard. Then, as if from far away, he heard his wife scream.

Ahead he saw a tiny speckle of land floating alone in the waters of the Caribbean. As the speck grew larger, he heard more gunfire, closer now.

Through the windshield he saw the propeller that had comforted him slow. Then the revolutions ceased entirely, and they began to drop faster.

The DEA man watched the tiny particle of land take shape, becoming an island. Tana screamed again, her fingers threatening to break his hand.

A split second later Gonzalez could make out green trees and bushes. Then the leaves and vines of the vegetation came into focus, and a heartbeat later he saw only the color green.

Then the shapeless green turned to an all-encompassing black.

Then Reuben Gonzalez saw nothing.

1

Below lay inescapable danger and probable death.

Blistering air struck Mack Bolan's face as he dived from the plane. The slipstream tugged him toward the tiny speck of green floating alone in the warm blue waters of the Caribbean. He glanced overhead and saw the plane become a tiny black spot against the clouds.

Bolan yanked the rip cord, and the chute flowered open above his head, jerking him upward momentarily as the canopy filled with air. Gripping the risers, he angled his descent toward the green core of the island.

A few minutes remained before touchdown, and he took advantage of the time, running a quick mental inventory of the equipment, both standard and special purpose, that hung from his tiger-striped jungle camouflage fatigues.

The sound-suppressed Beretta 93-R rode under his left arm in the well-worn shoulder rig; a Desert Eagle .44 Magnum was strapped to his right hip.

Both handguns were like body parts to the man known as the Executioner. He donned them habitually, with no more thought than most men give to their socks and shoes.

At the end of a sling in combat-carry mode, Bolan toted a Heckler & Koch MP-5 submachine gun. Canvas pouches, threaded through the belt of his combat harness, hid extra magazines for the sub and both handguns. A Cold Steel All Terrain Chopper—an updated version of the ancient Gurkha bush-fighting knife—hung from his belt in a leather sheath. Next to the Chopper was a small leather pouch containing a Leatherman Pocket Tool, a modern spin-off of the classic Swiss army knife.

The suspender straps of the combat harness had been decorated with six grenades—three frag, three smokers. A small black nylon buttpack held his compass and miscellaneous other items.

The Executioner studied the terrain below as he fell through the sky, hoping the long shot might come through and he'd spot his target from the air. Instead, an amalgamation of dense jungle broken by swampy marshes met his eyes. He reviewed what he'd learned of the island during the quick flight from Miami.

Grand Cayman, the capital island of the three Cayman Islands, survived because of two industries— tourism and the Cayman Turtle Farm, breeding sea turtles and manufacturing tortoise products. It was a small fleck of land set atop the ocean approximately one hundred ninety miles south of Cuba and northwest of Jamaica.

The island's larger east side was made up of scattered villages surrounding the coast. The interior consisted of the jungle and swampland Bolan now saw from the air.

The warrior tugged at the risers again, swaying in the Caribbean breeze and angling toward a swampy clearing near the center of the jungle.

Still three hundred feet from the ground, he saw the four men.

Creeping along the edge of the foliage next to the clearing, the men moved slowly, pausing occasionally to peer around the mangroves. Bolan recognized the distinct lines of an AK-47 in the hands of one man, an Uzi gripped in the fists of another. They wore street clothes, a sure sign that they'd come quickly, without adequate preparation.

That told the Executioner one thing. These men were the enemy.

Bolan's right hand found the grip of the MP-5. The breeze guiding his chute was light, and he was too low to alter course now. His eyes scanned the small square of open land.

The men were to his left. The nearest cover would be the trees, directly ahead of where he'd land.

So far, they hadn't spotted him.

Bolan thumbed the safety to full-auto as he continued his descent.

So much for coming in low profile.

A hundred feet from the ground, a man wearing a sweat-stained white dress shirt looked up from the trees. He had just enough time to raise his Uzi before the Executioner tapped the trigger of the MP-5.

A steady stream of full-auto 9 mm slugs shredded through the white shirt.

The other three men jerked their heads up. Bolan cut a figure eight back and forth between two of them, his rounds ripping through the leaves and vines to stop them in their tracks.

Still twenty feet in the air, the Executioner dropped the H&K to the end of the sling and reached up, popping the chute's quick-release harnesses. The clank of a closing Thompson bolt resounded below. Then stuttering, slow-paced gunfire flew over the warrior's head and through the fluttering chute.

Bolan rolled onto a shoulder as he hit the soggy ground. Mud flew in clumps as he came to a halt on his belly and sighted through the O-ring sight on top of the MP-5.

The man with the Thompson ducked deeper into the dense vegetation.

Rolling to his feet, the Executioner sprinted toward the trees. More rounds burst from the jungle, splattering wetly into the marsh around his feet. He hit the ground again, returned fire, then sprinted off once more, zigzagging toward cover.

A short burst pursued him. Then, in the silence that followed, he heard a string of Spanish curses; metallic clicks echoed through the trees as the man with the Thompson fumbled to insert a fresh mag into his weapon.

Bolan twisted as he ran, firing blindly in the general direction from which the rounds had come, and heard a low moan as he dived headfirst into the undergrowth.

He rammed a new clip into the MP-5 and switched the safety to semiautomatic.

Still on his belly, Bolan crawled slowly through the foliage, angling toward the spot where the men had been. He moved slowly, silently, making his way through a wild patch of bright red bougainvillea.

With the gunfire absent, the usual buzzing noises of the jungle began to return. Exotic birds—blue-winged parrots and black ching-chings—flew overhead to light in the branches of the tall royal palms. Mosquitoes buzzed in hordes, stinging his face and arms as they drew the blood from his body like tiny vampires.

Ten minutes later the Executioner heard a faint slapping sound. He froze, the H&K extended in front of him. A few seconds later he heard another slap, then the soft crunch of a damp twig under a shoe.

The odor of stale cigarettes wafted toward him on the breeze.

Bolan saw a flicker of movement through the vines. He rose to one knee, peering between the leaves to see the man with the Thompson.

Bright crimson dripped steadily from a wound on the side of the man's neck. Mosquitoes had swarmed to the blood like sharks in a feeding frenzy. Misery flowed from the subgunner's eyes as he gave in to the itch, frantically slapping the insects from the wound.

Bolan rose to his feet. The man with the Thompson turned toward the movement, and the Executioner squeezed the trigger of his MP-5, sending a lone 9 mm to ease the guy's discomfort forever.

The Executioner moved swiftly through the jungle, quickly surveying the rest of the corpses, and he found exactly what he'd expected to find. Each man wore slacks and a sport shirt, clothing more fitting to the street than the jungle.

No, these men hadn't planned to end up in the bush when they dressed that morning. Ties still hung from the necks of two of the men.

The hunters were dark complected, obviously Hispanic. They had to be Peruvian, gunners for the Lima drug cartel.

The warrior returned to the clearing. The parachute had finally settled twenty yards to the east, the nylon canopy snagging in the branches of a white mangrove. Bolan drew his knife, cut the chute from the tree and buried it in the soft, wet mud.

Pulling the compass from his buttpack, he took a quick reading, then headed east across the clearing. The Executioner had no idea in what part of the jungle the DEA plane had crashed, but if they'd come from Peru, they'd have approached from that direction. So from that direction he would start.

Brognola's quick briefing had told him only that one of the DEA agents had gotten off a radio transmission after the crash. The message had been picked up by the Cayman Island police and relayed to U.S. Customs. Customs had contacted the Justice Department.

The message was simple. Two of the agents had died in the crash. Reuben Gonzalez had been injured, but he and his wife, Tana, were both alive.

Bolan left the clearing and entered the jungle once more, slashing a path through the dense undergrowth as he went. According to Brognola, the Cayman Island authorities had relayed the message only as a courtesy. They wanted no American help in locating the wreckage. Even Brognola's warnings that the Lima cartel would stop at nothing to assure themselves of Gonzalez's silence hadn't persuaded them to accept the offer of American assistance.

Sweat broke out on Bolan's forehead. The jacket of his fatigue blouse stuck to his chest as he continued through the jungle.

Already the Peruvian cartel had men on the island, well-armed killers who'd do anything necessary to stop Gonzalez from bringing indictments and testifying against their bosses.

Unless Gonzalez and his wife were located and removed to America immediately, all hell would break loose on Grand Cayman.

Bolan came to the edge of another marsh. He paused, assured himself he was still alone, then crossed quickly into the trees on the other side.

Grand Cayman had no hope of protecting the Gonzalezes from an organization like the Lima cartel. And the island itself might not survive the carnage that would take place as the Peruvian hit men searched for the DEA agent and his wife. The Caymans had no military, only a small, unarmed police force with no experience at dealing with the type of killers they were about to encounter.

The Cayman Islands, and Reuben and Tana Gonzalez, had only the Executioner.

THE SWAMPLAND BECAME more sparse, the spotty mangroves and buttonwood trees giving way to thicker herbage as Bolan neared Grand Cayman's east end.

An open area of low growth separated him from the highway ringing the island. Far in the distance, on the other side of the road, stood several buildings and a radio tower. Farther south the aged stones of an ancient obelisk emerged from the shoreline. Halfway in between, a quarter mile out on the reef, sat the wrecked remnants of a rusting Nazi gunboat.

Bolan pulled the map from his buttpack. The tower was Radio Cayman, the stone spire Gorling Bluff Lighthouse. He was at Sparrowhawk Point, the southeast corner of the island.

The Executioner folded the map back into his pack. Sticking to the edge of the forest, he followed the compass due north until he reached the tiny village of Collier's. When the lines of the Tortuga Club took shape on the shore, he faced the ocean.

Using the compass, Bolan estimated the DEA plane's probable angle of flight, then charted a course back through the jungle.

The warrior sliced his way once more through tangled vines, and slogged ankle deep through the mud of the marshes. It was almost noon when he saw the first signs of the crash. The tops of several cedar trees had been clipped by the descending craft. Broken boughs dangled overhead, and fresh splinters of wood had fallen to the forest floor.

Bolan slung the H&K and drew the Beretta. Thumbing the fire selector to 3-round burst, he cautiously followed the trail of the descending aircraft.

As he neared another swamp area, the sound of voices swept to him through the trees.

Twenty feet away four men sprawled in exhaustion across the mud. Their weapons—assault rifles and submachine guns—had been dropped haphazardly to the ground at their sides.

A thin, dark man with graying temples sat facing the Executioner. He tipped a plastic canteen to his lips, then handed it to the man at his side. "You didn't know when Mr. Mariategui hired you that you'd be a hunter, eh, Pablo?" he said sarcastically in Spanish.

A rotund man with a two-day growth of beard stopped scraping mud from his loafers with a stag-handled hunting knife. He took the canteen and slurped loudly, his fleshy jowls quivering. The fat man's face showed the strain and fatigue of unaccustomed exertion as he passed on the canteen. "I enjoy hunting," he said. "But I usually don't hunt what I can't eat."

At the center of the group sat a cartel gunman, wearing an unbuttoned, mud-streaked white dress shirt. "Pablo," he said, "your bowie." He indicated the stag-handled knife. Hairy rolls of fat rippled over his belt buckle as he leaned forward to take the weapon. Scraping the blade lightly across a scrap of newspaper in his lap, he clumsily attempted to gather white powder in the center. He cursed as the paper dipped to an angle and the fine grains of cocaine fell to the ground.

Bolan ducked as the man with the gray temples suddenly looked up. The older man turned toward him, studying the leaves for a moment, then turned his eyes back to the group.

The Executioner flipped the Beretta to semiauto and checked to make sure the suppressor was screwed tightly into the barrel. He didn't know how far away the crash site was, but these men had to be nearing it. Other search parties might be, too.

This was no time to announce his presence.

Bolan sighted down the barrel, aiming the 93-R through a break in the greenery. The older man seemed the only one on alert. Resting the front sight on one of the gray temples, the Executioner squeezed the trigger.

A round red hole appeared through the gray. The older man sat motionless, blank eyes staring ahead.

The warrior turned the Beretta on the fat man and squeezed again. Blood gushed from just below the man's left eye.

The other two men jumped up in surprise, both reaching for Uzis on the ground next to them.

Bolan rose and dropped the sights on the gunner with the floral shirt. He tapped two rounds from the Beretta, taking the young man out of play before he could reach his subgun.

The man cutting the cocaine threw the hunting knife toward the trees, the blade flipping end over end three feet to the Executioner's side. As he stooped to the mud for his Uzi, Bolan fired again, a single 9 mm round tearing into the chest, punching him to the ground.

The Executioner stepped from the clearing, glanced down and walked on.

Singed leaves and vines, the result of the plane's exhaust, led him the rest of the way to the Beechcraft. Bolan stared through the trees into a small marsh break, seeing a mangled mass of metal.

Mud coated the contorted steel of the wings where they'd furrowed deeply through the swamp. Around the mud the warrior could see bullet holes in the plane's thin skin. Some of the holes looked to have come from hand guns, machine pistols or assault rifles. Others were far too large to be the result of small-arms fire.

The Executioner thought back to Brognola's quick briefing on the Lima cartel. DEA Intel reported rumors of a recently acquired black-market RAF Phantom, equipped with an M-61 Vulcan pod, multibarrel machine gun. He stared at the massive holes in the body of the Beechcraft. What had been rumor could now enter the DEA files as fact.

The warrior wiped sweat from his forehead with the back of his sleeve and surveyed the clearing. The DEA pilot had done an extraordinary job, guiding his craft to the only decent place to land.

Still, it hadn't been enough.

Bolan reholstered the Beretta, gripped the H&K and stepped from the trees. Halfway to the plane he spotted scattered 9 mm brass. Some of it sat high, on top of the mud; some had been trampled into the wet soil.

The Executioner squatted briefly, studying the footprints. Next to one set was the impression of a palm that had caught the weight of its falling body, and the telltale heel prints of bodies being dragged.

Bolan followed the tracks back to the edge of the forest, coming upon two bodies hastily concealed near the tree line. An Uzi and a MAC-10 machine pistol had been dropped next to them.

Two more cartel gunners down for the count.

The Executioner hurried back to the plane, ducking to squeeze through the twisted door. Inside he found two more bodies. Webber, Brognola had told him, and Rainey.

Bolan checked briefly under both men's jackets. SIG-Sauer automatics still rode in their holsters.

The rear seats of the Baron had been ripped from their struts by the force of the crash. They rested six inches from where Webber and Rainey still sat.

Dried blood splattered the floor and backs of the front seats. Otherwise, there was no sign of Reuben or Tana Gonzalez.

The warrior frowned as he summed up the evidence. After the crash Reuben Gonzalez had still been capable of defending himself from the attacking cartel men, and he'd had the presence of mind to hide the bodies.

But he hadn't had the foresight to add the other agents' weapons to his arsenal before fleeing the scene.

Bolan leaned forward and gently closed the eyes of the two men. He stepped down from the plane and followed two sets of tracks to the southwest edge of the clearing.

THE HOT TROPICAL SUN beat down through the trees, mixed with the humid air and created an almost unbearable heat. Large beads of sweat materialized on Bolan's face, running in tiny rivulets from his forehead down his nose to sting his eyes. He pulled a camouflage bandanna from his pack, rolled it into a headband and tied it above his ears. Continuing through the green hell of the interior of Grand Cayman, he ignored the mosquitoes and other insects that feasted on his face and neck.

The Executioner watched the ground as he sloshed through the swamps, following the muddy tracks. A short, light person was half carrying an individual with larger feet. Now and then, other indentations appeared in the mud—a palm print, a knee or an elbow, where one or both of the fleeing figures had slipped and fallen.

Small red dashes of blood stood out in bold relief against an occasional leaf that had blown from the jungle areas. Reuben Gonzalez was injured, and his wife had her hands full.

Entering another of the sporadic forests, Bolan drew the Chopper and cut his way through the vegetation, following the broken vines and branches the Gonzalezes had left in passing.

The blood spots became more frequent. The bright red splotches fell more vertically now, indicating that the couple's speed had slowed. Whether the declining pace came more from the thicker vegetation or Reuben's injury, Bolan had no way of knowing.

What he *did* know was that the blood was fresher. He was closing the gap.

Approaching another clearing, the Executioner heard muffled voices in the distance. He crouched, creeping quietly through the dense vegetation as the sounds became louder. Angry men were arguing in Spanish.

"Julio, I'm in charge. *I'll* be first."

"*I* found her."

The Executioner dropped to his hands and knees, crawling through the tangled undergrowth as the arguing continued.

"The hell with both of you. No one will have her. We haven't come to rape women. We've been sent to kill a traitor."

Bolan increased his speed, moving quickly and soundlessly from tree to tree.

"You're right, Juan," another voice said. "We have work to do. But why not combine business with pleasure?"

The Executioner reached the edge of the swamp and crawled quickly behind a large boulder. The vines rustled with his movement.

"What was that?"

"Nothing, Juan. A parrot. Maybe a lizard."

Bolan raised his head, peering through the leaves.

A tall gaunt man gripping a MAC-10 turned to a shorter man with a wispy Charlie Chan mustache. The tall figure dropped his free hand to his crotch and squeezed. "Where are your balls, Marco?" he asked. His eyes opened wide in mock realization. "Ah," he said. "Excuse me. I understand. It's the *man* you'd rather have, eh?"

Raucous laughter echoed through the clearing.

In addition to the tall man and the one with the drooping mustache, three more cartel gunners stood ankle deep in mud at the center of the clearing. Besides the Ingram, three of the men carried short-barreled, pump-action shotguns. The other cradled a Valmet M78 assault rifle in the crook of his arm.

Directly behind them, tied back to back to the trunk of a tall tree, Bolan saw the Gonzalezes. Blood dripped from the agent's forehead as he struggled furiously against the ropes that bound his hands to his sides. His wife stared dully across the clearing, her face a blank mask of hysteric disbelief.

As the laughter abated, the man with the wispy mustache spoke. "You're the pervert, Julio." He slung the Valmet over his shoulder and turned toward the woman. "I'll have her first—so you'll know what to do." He moved toward the tree.

The others followed, turning their backs toward Bolan. Slowly the Executioner rose.

"What of our old friend Cha-cha?" Julio called after him. He motioned toward Gonzalez with the MAC-10.

"Let him watch," he said. "It'll be the last thing he sees."

Reuben grappled harder against his restraints, a long stream of curses pouring from his lips. "No!" he shouted. "I'll kill all of you bastards!"

Marco slapped him across the face. "Silence, traitor, or you'll die now."

Bolan levelled the front sights of the MP-5 on Marco as the five gunmen formed a ring around Tana. The warrior's finger tightened on the trigger, then relaxed.

Positioned against the tree, on the other side of Marco, Tana Gonzalez stood directly in the Executioner's line of fire.

The H&K was filled with hot-load 9 mm slugs that would not only penetrate Marco's body, but hers, as well. Regardless of how well the shots were placed, the light 95-grain bullets could deflect off bone, or even muscle, change course and plow through the cartel gunner into Tana.

Slowly Bolan ducked back down and moved to his right, hearing the damp leaves and twigs rustle quietly with the movement. From the clearing he heard the rip of clothing, then a soft whimper. Then a high, feminine voice said, "Please... No..."

The Executioner heard more laughter as he glanced through the tangled vines. The man called Marco held the remnants of the woman's blouse in his hand. He stood transfixed, staring down at the soft white flesh barely contained by her bra.

Out of sight to the side, Reuben cursed again.

Bolan frowned. His angle of fire was still no good. Another two feet or so...

Marco pulled a lock blade folding knife from a pouch on his belt, flipped it open with one hand and slowly cut through one bra strap.

The warrior moved another foot to the left and glanced back through the foliage. Seeing that both Tana and Reuben were now clear, he raised the H&K once more.

Marco took a step to one side to cut the other strap.

And put her back in the line of fire.

Suddenly Reuben Gonzalez ripped one hand free and lunged for Marco. The tall man stepped back and lifted the knife. Grinning evilly, he taunted, "Ah, Cha-cha. You don't care to watch? Perhaps you're afraid she'll enjoy it more with us than you, no?" He paused, and the grin faded. "I'll grant you your wish. You won't have to watch, man. You'll die *now*."

Marco pulled the Valmet over his shoulder and stuck the barrel under Reuben's chin.

Both Tana and her husband were still too close, but it all became academic. It was a calculated risk he'd have to take. He had no more time.

Rising to his feet, the Executioner stepped into the clearing.

SHARP PAINS SHOT THROUGH Marino Mariategui's chest. He felt the sour, acidlike burn rise from his stomach to his throat. No, he reminded himself. It wasn't his heart.

The doctor had called them anxiety attacks, brought on by too much stress.

Mariategui held the steaming cup of coffee to his lips, touched his tongue gingerly to the rim, then set it back on the coaster in front of him. Still too hot.

Nervously he rubbed his chin, feeling the thick scar tissue—the result of a knife fight in Bogotá when he was a youth—that ran down the side of his face. He shifted on the couch, crossing his left leg over his right, and glanced toward the massive oak desk at the center of Hector Pizarro's outer office.

Lola, Pizarro's busty secretary, had finished filing her nails. She now worked expertly at applying a light violet polish to the end of her long fingers. The woman had been engaged in similar insignificant pursuits ever since he'd arrived more than fifteen minutes ago.

Mariategui's eyes fell instinctively to the long slim legs that extended from Lola's short cotton skirt. High on her thigh he could see the plastic snap that fastened the sheer tan nylons to a white garter belt.

He sighed quietly. He'd never met Lola before, but he *had* seen Pizarro's fat wife. His superior hadn't hired this breathtaking goddess for her typing ability.

Mariategui stared out the window, his thoughts turning to Jesús Pasquela. Cha-cha.

Or as he now knew the man, Reuben Gonzalez.

Anger flooded through him as he recalled the reason Pizarro had called him to the office—Cha-cha. Mariategui's brother-in-law had introduced him to Cha-cha three years ago. The face had been familiar, and they soon remembered they'd met years earlier in Colombia when they both worked for General Juan Montoya and the Medellín cartel.

He and Cha-cha had quickly become like brothers, bonding together in one of those instant camaraderies that came so rarely once a man reached adulthood. They'd eaten together, hunted in the Andes and fished the waters of the Amazon.

Ah, and Cha-cha had been . . . smooth. He'd never approached Mariategui for work, but rather had waited until the midlevel cartel boss asked *him* if he was interested.

Mariategui popped another antacid tablet as flames shot through his abdomen. His hand returned to his face, unconsciously tracing the line of the old knife wound.

He'd trusted Jesús Pasquela and had run the cartel's usual in-depth background check only because it was required. He'd found that Jesús Pasquela was who he said he was—an American of Hispanic descent who the National Crime Information Center listed as having been arrested four times for narcotics trafficking. One conviction, and a two-year stint in the federal penitentiary at El Reno, Oklahoma.

For two years he and Cha-cha had worked side by side, arranging cocaine shipments to America, Europe, even the Orient. The little American had quickly endeared himself to the ranking members of the cartel—even to Hector Pizarro himself.

Mariategui pulled a handkerchief from his pocket and mopped at his forehead. If not for the sudden arrival of the blond woman, he might still not know the truth.

The buzzer on Lola's desk suddenly sounded, starting Mariategui from his reverie.

The woman reluctantly set down her nail brush and lifted the receiver. "Yes?" She listened for a moment, then replaced the receiver in the cradle and turned toward him. "You may go in."

Mariategui rose unsteadily, his legs feeling as if they were directed by remote control. He raised his hand to knock, then lowered it. No. Go in, she'd said.

Hands clasped behind his back, Hector Pizarro stood at the rear of the elaborately decorated office. The short flabby man faced away from the door, toward the huge, water-filled aquarium that stretched the length of the back wall.

Several dozen piranhas swam lazily back and forth behind the glass. Razor-tipped teeth extended from their lipless mouths and sparkled through the lighted water. Their dead eyes stared dully ahead as they drifted aimlessly throughout the tank.

A large glass fishbowl sat on a table in front of the tank. Inside were several goldfish.

Without turning around, Pizarro said, "Sit down, Marino."

Mariategui moved across the carpet to a straight-backed wooden chair facing the desk. As soon as he sat, he felt himself slide toward the front of the seat. Bracing his legs, he shoved himself back against the rest.

He relaxed and began to slide again.

Mariategui glanced to the floor. The front legs of the chair had been shortened—just enough to make sitting in it an uncomfortable and unnerving experience.

Just enough to aid in the psychological intimidation that was the trademark of Hector Pizarro.

Mariategui looked up as his boss turned to him and smiled. The fat man's voice wheezed slightly as he spoke. "I never tire of watching the piranhas. They are simple fish. Primitive. Uncomplicated. They think only of food and mating. They know what they want . . . and they take it." He stooped slightly behind the desk. When he rose, he held a small net in his right hand.

Dipping the net into the goldfish bowl, Pizarro lifted several of the unsuspecting creatures into the air. "Alone, Marino," the cartel boss continued, "the piranha need not be feared. But they know that in numbers there's strength. Together a school of piranhas can quickly destroy far larger fish, animals, even the unfortunate human who chances to be in the water at the wrong place and time." Pizarro turned toward the aquarium. "Observe."

He lifted the net high into the air and dropped four goldfish in with the piranhas.

"Hector—" Mariategui began.

Pizarro held up a hand, silencing him, and pointed to the aquarium.

For a moment the goldfish darted through the water, swimming erratically in terrified bursts, seeking escape. Then suddenly, in a flurry of splashes, the orange-bellied meat-eaters converged.

Faster than the eye could follow, the piranhas seemed to work in tandem, one fish snapping the rear half of each goldfish between its jaws before backing off and allowing its partner to gulp the rest.

In less than a second all four goldfish had disappeared, and the piranhas returned to their idle circling.

Pizarro took a seat behind the desk. The smile that had covered his portly face disappeared. "Marino," he said, "we have a very serious problem."

"Hector, if you will allow me to explain—"

Again Pizarro held up his hand, and Mariategui felt a chill rush through his body. Power—the power of literal life and death—radiated from the Lima cartel boss's eyes.

"I'll make our meeting short, Marino," Pizarro continued. "Time is of the essence. Your friend Chacha has no evidence that could endanger me personally, but I don't intend to stand idly by while he disrupts our operation. *You* will fly immediately to Grand

Cayman and oversee the search. Pasquela—Gonzalez—whoever he may actually be—isn't to reach America." He paused, taking a deep, wheezing breath. "Take however many men and whatever arms you feel you'll need."

Mariategui nodded. "He'll be found." He tried to clear his throat, but whatever blocked it didn't budge. "May I ask a foolish question?"

"Considering your actions to this point, it would seem appropriate, Marino."

"As you know, the traitor was introduced to me by my sister's husband...."

Pizarro nodded slowly. "Unknown to us, your brother-in-law was arrested four years ago by DEA agents. He was freed with the understanding that he'd assist them."

"Yes," Mariategui said. "Everything begins to fall into place. And what, if I may ask, will become of Santos?"

Pizarro stared at him. "He's no longer a piranha, Marino. He has become a goldfish. My condolences to your sister."

Mariategui felt the blood drain from his face. Slowly he forced himself to nod and rose to his feet.

"Before you go, I'd like to show you what happens when a piranha becomes weak." The cartel boss pulled a small knife from his pocket and opened the blade. Then, dipping the net into the tank, he removed one of the hand-sized killer fish. As the piranha flipped in the net, Pizarro made a quick slash across its belly, then tossed it into the tank.

The other fish attacked, and in a swift orgy of teeth, blood and churning water, the wounded piranha disappeared as quickly as had the goldfish.

His legs like lead, Mariategui started for the door. As his shaking hand twisted the knob, he heard Pizarro's voice. "I've always liked you, Marino. You've served well in your job."

The cartel boss cleared his throat. "Find Gonzalez," he said. "You're not a goldfish like your brother-in-law, Santos." He paused again. Then, with the power of life and death in his voice once more, he said, "But don't become an injured piranha, either, my friend."

2

The Executioner's first burst drilled through Marco's mustache, obliterating the lower half of his face.

The other four cartel gunners turned toward Bolan in shock.

A man wearing an expensive straw panama hat raised his shotgun, jacking the slide along the barrel to chamber a round. The sound echoed hollowly above the declining whine of the MP-5.

The warrior turned the H&K on the pump gunner, depressed the trigger and sent a steady stream of parabellums chopping through his flesh. The panama and the shotgun fell to the ground as the man's body jerked in convulsions, then dropped in a heap.

The other shotgun boomed, and the Executioner felt a lone pellet rip into his upper arm, heard a tiny ping as yet another ricocheted off one of the grenades that hung from his battle harness.

The warrior whipped the barrel of the MP-5 toward the second shotgunner, two rounds from a triburst glancing off the shotgun's receiver and into the tree next to Tana's head. The woman screamed in terror.

Bolan's third round bore through the shotgun's wooden stock, then entered the gunner's rib cage. The man's screams rivaled Tana's as the pump gun went flying from his hands.

The man with the MAC-10 broke from the group and fled toward the jungle, twenty yards away.

The Executioner dived to the marshy ground, rolling to one side as two loads of 12-gauge buckshot burst from the barrel of the last shotgun. Mud and grass exploded to his side. He rolled back toward the flying earth as the man with the pump gun adjusted his aim and let loose again. Coming to a halt on his stomach, the warrior sent two 9 mm rounds into the hardguy's knees.

Turning quickly, Bolan took time for a snap shot at the man racing for the cover of the jungle, the round sailing high over the man's shoulder.

From the corner of his eye, the Executioner saw the knee-shot gunman fall to a sitting position in the mud, his shotgun stabbing barrel down into the soggy soil.

Bolan fired again as the fleeing gunner reached the edge of the trees. The man dropped the MAC-10 and shrieked as blood gushed from a hole in the back of his thigh. Grasping the back of his leg as if he'd just pulled a hamstring muscle, he disappeared into the foliage.

The warrior turned back to the shotgunner. The cartel killer's eyes burned with hatred as he raised the mud-clogged barrel of his weapon and jerked the trigger.

The blocked barrel cracked and exploded, sending shrapnel tearing through the gunman's face, chest and arms. Flames danced from the breech, lapping up through billows of smoke as the man screamed in agony.

The Executioner pulled the trigger of the MP-5, a 3-round burst ending the gunner's pain.

Bolan glanced toward Reuben and Tana Gonzalez, still tied to the tree. "I'll be back," he said, then shoved a fresh magazine into the H&K and sprinted toward the jungle.

He leapt over the fallen MAC-10, then slowed his pace as he followed the steady trail of fresh blood through the tangled vines. Red spots splattered in ever-increasing dimensions, the blood from the thigh wound splashing steadily with the fleeing man's every step.

Somewhere ahead Bolan heard him thrashing through the trees. The warrior quickened his pace. The gunfire was bound to have drawn the attention of other cartel search parties, but they'd have only a general idea of the shots' location.

This man could pinpoint Reuben and Tana exactly. He couldn't afford to let him escape.

Suddenly the thrashing ahead of him stopped. Bolan slowed, his battle-senses alert, searching the jungle for the slightest sound. He moved on, walking the thin line between too little speed and too much noise— noise that would give him away and allow the cartel man to set up an ambush.

The gunner had dropped the MAC-10 as he entered the jungle. It was the only weapon Bolan had spotted on him.

But that didn't mean it was the only weapon he had.

To his right Bolan suddenly saw a flurry of color as the vines parted. Bringing the MP-5 around in an arc, Bolan felt steel meet steel as the subgun barrel blocked the descending machete.

Bolan took a half step back as the man with the machete again raised the massive blade high overhead. The warrior raised the folding stock of the H&K and smashed it into the soft flesh of the cartel gunner's throat, stifling a scream.

Somewhere in the distance he heard the thrashing sounds of more men hurrying in their direction. Drawing the All Terrain Chopper, the warrior slashed the knife across his enemy's throat, then eased the body to the matted jungle floor.

Bolan took off, back toward the Gonzalezes.

Reaching the marshy clearing, he slogged through the mud to the tall fir tree. Tana continued to stare ahead, as if in a trance. Reuben's face grimaced in pain as the hand he'd already freed worked at the knots that still held him.

The Executioner slung the MP-5 when he reached them.

Reuben looked up. "Who are you?"

Bolan didn't answer. He drew his knife and cut through the ropes. The DEA agent slumped to a sitting position on the ground, new pain registering on his face. His hand shot to his hip.

The warrior moved to the other side of the tree, and Tana turned toward him, her face a vacant mask. He swung the Chopper again, slicing neatly through the ropes that bound her arms and legs to the tree trunk.

He grasped her chin gently in his hand and looked into her eyes.

"Can you hear me?" he asked.

Slowly the woman nodded.

"We're not out of it yet. Can you walk?" he asked the DEA agent.

Reuben took a deep breath. "Some. My hip might be broken."

Bolan looked into the jungle. Vines and leaves whipped and snapped as the searchers neared.

He turned back to Reuben. "Okay. We don't have time to fix you up now. We're about to have more visitors. I'll take care of them, then we've got to get out of here, quick. This place is alive with hostiles."

He turned back to Tana. "Give me a hand."

As the Executioner lifted Reuben to his feet, Tana continued to gape as if hypnotized. "Come on," Bolan ordered. "I need your help." Slowly she moved toward her husband.

The warrior needed no help moving Reuben. The man stood maybe five-nine and couldn't have weighed more than one-sixty.

But the woman appeared in need of help. She was in shock, and Bolan knew he had to keep her busy. He had to get her out of the zombielike state the unaccustomed violence had produced.

If he didn't, he'd have two people to carry instead of one.

Bolan grabbed the Valmet from the ground and handed it to Reuben. The DEA man limped in pain as the Executioner half carried him to the jungle on the opposite side of the marshland. Tana followed.

Positioning them both low in the undergrowth, Bolan said, "Stay down." He turned to Reuben. "Don't give away your position. Don't fire unless I get hit. You got it?"

The agent nodded.

Bolan hurried back to the clearing, dropping onto his side on the ground just in front of the tree. He set the MP-5 in front of his outstretched hand, the grip facing his opened fingers. As he heard the first of the men reach the clearing, he yanked the Beretta from the shoulder rig, holding it hidden under his body in his left hand. Eyes opened wide as if frozen in sudden death, the Executioner relaxed the other muscles of his body.

One of the largest men Bolan had ever seen stepped cautiously into the clearing. The hardguy's fingers tightened around an AK-47, and his mouth dropped open in surprise as he spotted the bodies on the ground.

Bolan strained to keep from blinking, his eyelids threatening to drop involuntarily. He had to wait. He'd heard at least three voices in the approaching search party. More men would come.

After what seemed like an eternity, two more cartel gunners stepped out of the brush and stood next to the giant.

"It's Marco," said a man wearing a red bandanna. "And Julio and Antonio. They're dead." He gestured toward the bodies with the short barrel of the Steyr AUG in his hands.

The giant nodded slowly, then pointed toward Bolan with the AK-47. "But they've killed the bastard who got them."

"Yes," one of the other gunners said, "but where's Cha-cha and his woman?"

Bolan waited another few seconds. Then, confident that any other searchers who had accompanied these men would have already reached the clearing, he inched his fingers toward the H&K.

The man in the bandanna cleared his throat nervously, then turned to the giant. "What are we going to do, Miguel?"

The Executioner's fingers found the grip of the MP-5. "Try dying," he said, and swung the weapon toward the trio.

The surprised behemoth with the AK-47 lifted the rifle as the warrior fired, Bolan's 3-round burst stitching him from crotch to throat.

The warrior rose to one knee. With the H&K in his right hand, the Beretta in his left, he fired simultaneously. The man wearing the bandanna jerked convulsively as the MP-5 drilled a cracking burst of 9 mm slugs through his sternum; the bearded man fell to the ground as the Beretta did the same.

Assuring himself that the three men were dead, Bolan quickly gathered the weapons scattered throughout the clearing. Slinging the MAC-10 over his shoulder, he pulled three extra magazines from Marco's pockets and slid them into the pouches left empty by discarded MP-5 clips.

Reuben had passed out when Bolan returned to the jungle. He looked again at the gash across the DEA man's forehead. It was deep, but that area didn't bleed profusely. No, Reuben's unconsciousness more than likely came from fatigue and a possible concussion.

Bolan looked at Tana. The frail woman's eyes had clouded over. Physically she sat there in the jungle of Grand Cayman, her hand holding that of her sleeping husband. Mentally Tana Gonzalez was a thousand miles away.

The Executioner shook his head. He'd seen the symptoms before in people who'd suddenly been exposed to the stress of violence they weren't mentally prepared to deal with.

Call it battle fatigue, shell shock, whatever you wanted to. It all boiled down to the same thing—unless he could bring Tana out of it soon, he'd have a mental case to get to safety, as well as a wounded man.

But now wasn't the time. More cartel gunners would already be on their way. He, Reuben and Tana had to get out of there, and they had to do it fast.

He shook Reuben to consciousness and pulled him to his feet. Wrapping one of the man's arms around his shoulders, he turned back to Tana. "Let's go."

Tana fell in behind them.

It was rough going through the dense foliage. Bolan towed the DEA man with one arm and chopped at the vines with the other. He kept one eye on the woman a few feet behind them, making sure she kept up.

They came to another swampy clearing, crossed quickly and entered denser foliage on the other side. As they approached a small break in the vegetation, the Executioner glanced at Reuben's head wound. The bleeding had increased.

Bolan glanced behind him. They were several hundred yards from the site of the ambush, and he'd heard no sounds of pursuit as they made their way through the jungle.

It was time to let them rest, dress Reuben's wounds and try to get Tana out of her walking stupor.

The Executioner lowered Reuben to the ground, positioning him on his back. The DEA man's chest sucked in and out, gasping for oxygen. Bolan turned to Tana. "Stay here."

The woman took a seat on the leaves next to her husband.

Resheathing his knife, Bolan bent the vines out of his way as he made his way through the foliage. He wanted no telltale chop marks in the vegetation to point the way to where his charges were concealed.

When he was forty yards away, he stopped and withdrew the knife, hacking at the limbs and vines until he had all the vegetation he could carry.

Returning to where he'd left the Gonzalezes, he began threading the natural camouflage through the already thick foliage, creating a green "cocoon" that completely hid them from view.

Reuben looked up, raising his head slightly as the Executioner worked. "You're . . . you're not DEA."

"No."

"Who are you, then?"

The warrior paused and looked down at the man on the ground. "A friend."

"Justice Department?"

Bolan shrugged and went back to work. "Sort of. Rest now."

Gonzalez fell back to the leaves in exhaustion. "What do I call you?"

"Belasko will do."

Bolan finished the cocoon and knelt next to Reuben. He pulled a first-aid kit from his buttpack, set it on the ground next to the man and pulled the canteen from his belt. Taking another camouflage bandanna from the pack, he carefully cleaned the blood from the agent's head wound.

"You remember how it happened?" he asked the man.

Gonzalez shook his head. "Sometime during the crash," he said. "Hit ... something."

"How do you feel?"

"Dizzy sometimes. A little bit of a headache. Not too bad."

"Concussion?"

"I don't think so. No."

Bolan frowned. He wasn't so sure about that. The periodic dizziness wasn't a good sign, and the man's speech drifted from coherent to slurred.

The Executioner began applying a topical antiseptic to the gash. "How about the hip? Can you go on?"

Gonzalez shrugged. "Sure." He smiled weakly, then looked toward his wife. "But I'm just going to slow you down. Take *her,* Belasko. Please. Get her to safety."

Bolan shook his head. "Wrong, soldier. We *all* walk out of here. Or none of us do."

The man started to speak, but Bolan cut him off. "Relax. We'll make it."

Gonzalez's jaw tightened, showing the strain and confusion the man had already encountered and the uncertainty he was experiencing now. "How are we going to do that?"

"We've got a plane standing by at the airport. All we've got to do is get there."

"Can we do it?" the agent asked.

"Piece of cake." His face turned serious. "You need stitches. Think you can handle it?"

Reuben nodded slowly.

Bolan removed a surgical needle and thread from the first-aid kit. "Close your eyes. Try to think about something else. Take slow, steady breaths and concentrate on them."

Reuben closed his eyes and clenched his jaws, but no sounds escaped his lips.

The warrior finished the stitches and wound gauze around the agent's head, finishing with a tight layer of adhesive tape. He leaned back, frowning at the sharp contrast the white tape made against the green of the jungle. He might as well have painted a bull's-eye across the man's forehead.

Reaching into the pack once more, the warrior produced another cammo headband and tied it around the bandage.

Bolan quickly dressed the minor shotgun pellet wound on his upper arm, then turned back to Reuben. "You ready for the fun part?" he asked.

The man swallowed hard again. Without speaking, he nodded.

Bolan rolled him to his side, saw Reuben grit his teeth as he took hold of the waist and upper thigh. "Breathe deep a few times," he ordered.

The DEA agent had just let out the first breath when Bolan jerked on the leg. He heard a gritty, grinding sound as the joint snapped back into place.

A small shriek escaped Reuben's clenched teeth before he passed out once more.

Somewhere to the east the Executioner heard voices. The brush crackled as the unseen men made their way toward the green cocoon.

Bolan pressed Tana lower into the ground, covering her with his body. He unholstered the Beretta, flipped the fire selector to 3-round burst mode and waited.

Through the thick vegetation the Executioner watched as several men approached. A light blue color appeared, then green, then yellow. Bolan made out the ends of a loosened tie flapping near the tail of a dress shirt. Then the lapel of a light cotton sport coat passed the hole through which he looked.

Bolan counted four cartel gunners.

When the sounds of their passage had disappeared into the distance, the Executioner rose and helped Tana to a sitting position on the leaves. The woman's expression hadn't changed through the entire ordeal.

He took both of her hands in his, pressed his face close to hers and said, "Listen to me."

He got no response.

"Can you hear me?" he asked.

Tana nodded slowly.

"You've got to pull yourself out of this. You've been through a lot. You've seen things you've never seen before." He paused, hoping for a sign that his words were sinking in. He got nothing. "But we play the hand we're dealt, Mrs. Gonzalez. You've got to snap out of it or you'll die."

A faint smile crossed the woman's lips.

The Executioner took a deep breath. He'd seen that reaction to life-threatening situations before. There were people in the world whose only defense against unspeakable atrocities was withdrawal. When the horror got too bad, they retreated within themselves. Death no longer became a threat.

It became, in fact, a welcome end to the horror they were experiencing.

Bolan searched his mind. Somewhere within the woman, there was a reason why she'd want to live. Something she cared about. Something she would respond to.

He had to find it.

"Do you have children, Mrs. Gonzalez?" he asked.

Nothing. Just the same dull stare.

"Mrs. Gonzalez, your husband is dying."

Bolan saw a flicker of light flash in her pale blue eyes.

"Reuben is dying, Mrs. Gonzalez. He needs your help."

She turned slightly, looking deep into the eyes of the Executioner.

Bolan dropped her hands and reached up, rubbing her face. "Listen to me," he said again. "Reuben will die unless you help him."

Tana frowned. Her eyes began to focus on him. "Who are you?" she asked.

"I'm a friend, here to help you. To help you both."

"The men...the men with the guns...they wanted to kill..."

Bolan continued to rub her face. The pale white skin turned crimson as the blood rushed to the stimulated cheeks. "That's right. They wanted to kill you."

"Yes...Reuben and me...and...they were going to rape me."

"Yes. But they can't do that now," Bolan said. "We're leaving this place."

Tana's eyes opened wide. "And never coming back?"

"No. We'll never come back. But first we have to get out of here. Are you with me?"

Slowly Tana nodded and got to her feet.

He knelt once more and shook Reuben. The DEA man opened his weary eyes. "It's time to go," the Executioner told him.

Reuben turned toward his wife. "Is she all right?"

"Better. She'll improve as we go." Bolan pulled a square tin box from his buttpack and opened it, revealing individual compartments for black, brown and green camouflage makeup. He handed it to Reuben.

The DEA agent quickly smeared it across his face and hands, then turned to his wife. He gently covered her face with the makeup. Bolan saw him look down at her torn blouse and exposed bra. The DEA man finished with the makeup, handed the can back to the Executioner and began to unbutton his own shirt. He draped it around his wife's shoulders and buttoned it to the throat.

Tana smiled up at him, a new awareness entering her eyes.

"It'll be all right, honey," he promised. "Belasko will get us out of here."

Tana nodded. "I love you."

Reuben embraced her. "I love you, too."

As HE ROSE UNSTEADILY to his feet, Reuben Gonzalez watched Bolan pick up the Valmet M-78 and hand it to him. Reuben accepted the rifle and slung it over his shoulder, barrel forward, in the assault-carry mode he'd learned so long ago at the DEA Academy in Quantico, Virginia.

The agent almost laughed when Bolan extended the MAC-10 to Tana. She shrank from the weapon as if she'd been offered a poisonous snake.

Bolan shrugged, then turned and led them from the cover of the blind into the jungle.

Reuben limped along behind Bolan, his hand riding on the Valmet's grip. Yeah, the assault-carry mode, they'd called it. He'd learned it all right. But as an undercover agent, this was the first time he'd ever had to use it.

Sweat poured down his face. The deep, dull ache began again behind his eyes. He felt like having a cigarette, and he fished briefly through his pants pocket before remembering that he'd quit.

Fire seared through his relocated hip with every step, and the dizziness in his head came and went. He paused for a moment, grasping the limb of a scraggly tree as his equilibrium threatened to go completely.

Through fuzzy vision, Reuben saw the big man ahead of him turn and stare at him. He knew that the man was reevaluating his condition, wondering if he should carry him the rest of the way.

Reuben looked him in the eye and shook his head, answering the question before it could be asked. He shoved off from the limb and continued.

As they trudged along, the pain in Reuben's hip intensified. With it came the dull throbbing from the head wound.

He'd lied to Belasko. He *did* have a concussion. But he had to keep up, had to keep going on his own. If Belasko had to carry him, it wouldn't only slow them down, it would tie up the man's hands. His *gun* hands.

Tana would be in even more danger.

Finally Bolan halted. Reuben and Tana took seats on the jungle floor while he pulled a compass from his buttpack and flipped open the cover.

Reuben watched as the man squinted at the face of the instrument, and for the first time noticed the scars on his rescuer's face and hands. This man had seen action. He'd survived countless battles. The proof lay like an open book, printed across his skin.

A new confidence came over the DEA agent. If anyone could get them out of this situation and to safety, it would be this man called Belasko.

But who was he? A special agent? No, he'd said not. Was he a member of one of the newly formed Recon Arrest Teams—RATS—made up of Special Forces military personnel and led by DEA agents in the war on drugs?

Maybe. He had more the bearing of a soldier than anything else. Yet there was still something different about him.

Bolan closed the compass and dropped it back in his pack. "Ready?"

Reuben and Tana rose to their feet. "Who *are* you, Belasko?" Reuben asked again.

"The guy who's going to get you out of here, Reuben."

Gonzalez believed he meant it.

He hoped the big man was right.

3

Bolan collected vines and branches again as he led the Gonzalezes back toward the east end of the island. When the clear blue waters of the Caribbean finally peeked through the dense vegetation, the Executioner resheathed the Chopper and turned north, away from the giveaway trail the blade had left in their wake.

A hundred yards from the path he'd forged, Bolan stopped. There stood the Tortuga Club.

Bolan turned to Reuben and Tana as they both dropped to the ground in exhaustion. "I'll close you in, out of sight, then cross to the club." The warrior pointed through the trees, indicating the large building and smaller cottages across the highway. "We've got a man with a rented car waiting to pick us up as soon as I call. He'll fly us back to the U.S."

Reuben nodded. Tana opened her mouth to speak, then closed it.

"Go ahead, Mrs. Gonzalez," he said. "Tell me what's on your mind."

Slowly, her voice shaky, Tana said, "Then...we just stay here and wait?"

Bolan nodded.

"But what if they find us here?"

The warrior was encouraged. Not only was she aware of what was happening, but she was also beginning to question her own actions, realize she had to take responsibility for her own well-being. It was another good sign that the shock was wearing off.

"That's what these are for." The Executioner handed Reuben the Valmet, MAC and H&K. "And these." He held up the chopped foliage in his hands.

Bolan slid out of the battle harness and dropped it to the ground. Quickly he began threading the natural camouflage through the vines around the couple.

When he'd completed the new cocoon, Bolan stood outside the structure, staring through a tiny break in the vines. Reuben and Tana were barely visible. They'd be safe from all but the most careful, close-up scrutiny.

Stripping off his camouflage pants and blouse, the warrior turned them wrong-side out and slipped into them once more. The reversible khaki side resembled a safari suit. They were designed at Stony Man Farm, and the Executioner had been pleased to find that they did exactly what they were supposed to do, transform the jungle warrior quickly into a simple vacationer.

Pulling the bandanna from his forehead, Bolan removed the cammo makeup from his face, then stuffed the soiled cloth into his buttpack.

The pack wouldn't look out of place. Of simple black nylon, it wasn't an unlikely choice in which to carry a camera, film, or other travel necessities.

Bolan moved to the edge of the trees. Satisfied that the light traffic on the road were friendlies, he started across the clearing.

The Executioner thought about the Gonzalezes as he strolled casually toward the Tortuga Club. A lot was learned about people in life-and-death situations. Insights into personalities that took years to obtain under normal conditions often came in a heartbeat.

Reuben Gonzalez was one tough little guy. He'd gotten through the Executioner's stitch job without a word. He was strong willed, with a powerful survival instinct. And it was evident that the scrappy DEA agent had seen some action. Maybe not as concentrated as what he now faced, where every step became a battle of life and death, but he'd seen enough that he wasn't likely to fold under the pressure.

As long as he remained conscious and mobile, Gonzalez would be an asset rather than a liability. The operative phrase was "as long as." What concerned Bolan was the man's head wound. Gonzalez lost his balance too easily; he slipped where there was no mud; he grasped branches and trees for support.

The bottom line? Regardless of what the man said, he *did* have a concussion. How serious it was remained to be seen.

Reuben Gonzalez could be a walking time bomb.

Bolan reached the highway. Crossing the hot asphalt, he headed toward the closest entrance to the Tortuga Club Lounge.

Tana Gonzalez was another story. The fragile, pretty woman had obviously led the type of life most Americans enjoyed. Until the crash the most violent thing she'd ever been exposed to would be along the lines of a nasty paper cut.

Tana had no frame of reference to draw upon during this type of ordeal. She couldn't comprehend that there actually were people out there who would kill her without a moment's remorse.

As he neared the lounge, the Executioner stared at the waves lapping onto the beach. Scattered along the sand, the residents of the rental cottages relaxed on beach towels and aluminum recliners, oblivious to what was happening less than a mile away in the jungle.

Bolan pushed through the swinging glass door and entered the club. Behind a long teakwood bar, a bartender dressed in a white tux jacket, black T-shirt and blue jeans stood at the sink drying soap suds from highball glasses. To the bartender's side, a swing door with a triangular window led to what appeared to be the kitchen.

With the exception of the bartender, the Tortuga Club was deserted. The Executioner glanced at his watch. Midafternoon. The tourists were still at the beach, and it was too early for the natives to be off work.

The bartender looked up as Bolan entered. The warrior nodded, then crossed to the pay phone on the wall in the corner.

A tall bar stool had been pulled under the phone. Bolan took a seat, his back to the wall, and dialed the airport.

"Owen Roberts International Airport," a voice said.

"I'd like to page Mr. Bob Wolfe," Bolan stated, using the cover name he and Grimaldi had agreed on.

"One moment."

Bolan heard the PA system screech on and "Bob Wolfe" being paged.

Finally he heard Grimaldi's familiar voice. "Yeah, Striker. Ready when you are."

"I'm at the east end at a place called the Tortuga Club. It's on your map."

"Just a second."

Bolan listened, hearing the rustling of paper.

"Right. Got you pinpointed."

"Good. You've rented a car?"

"Ford LTD. Kind of a lime-yellow with some of the primer showing through on the driver's side. It shouldn't be hard to spot."

The Executioner glanced quickly around the bar, making certain there were no curious ears. "We're bivouacked in the boonies just west. I'm going back to wait with our 'package.' When you get here, don't park. Just drive slowly along the road. We'll be out to meet you."

"I'm on my way."

Bolan hung up. He was halfway off the stool when the picture window near the phone exploded.

Instinctively his hand shot under the khaki jacket, hauling the mammoth Desert Eagle .44 Magnum from hip leather. He dived to the floor as another explosion echoed through the room.

Bolan looked up to see two men carrying M-16s burst through the main door. He got off two Magnum rounds, dropping both men. Even as he fired, he heard commotion behind him.

A man wearing a light cotton three-piece suit leapt through the broken glass of the picture window, a nickel-plated Colt Python flashing in his hand.

The Executioner's first supersonic round zoomed through the gunner's vest before his feet hit the floor. The follow-up shot ripped the scalp from the top of the man's head. The shiny Python glimmered in the bar lights as it flew from the man's hand and he collapsed in a heap at Bolan's feet.

Through the shattered glass, the Executioner saw heads on the beach straining to see what was happening at the club. He jumped to his feet as two more Peruvian gunners entered from the highway side. He spun, his finger already tightening on the Desert Eagle's trigger, as a long burst of .223s sailed over his shoulder.

Bolan dropped to one knee as his trigger finger completed the pull. A booming round raced from the Desert Eagle's barrel and into the nose of a bald man firing a Ruger Mini-14.

Behind him a gunner with a handlebar mustache, wielding an Uzi, caught the blowout from the back of the bald man's head. He screamed in terror and abhorrence as blood, brains and bone fragments flew into his eyes.

The Executioner rose to his feet and sent a double-tap of .44s plummeting through the blinded man's chest. The 240-grain hollowpoints sent him rocketing back through the door through which he'd entered.

Suddenly all was quiet.

Bolan turned quickly toward the beach. Several sun worshipers stood staring at the club, unable to comprehend what was happening inside. He ejected the partial magazine from the Desert Eagle and rammed a fresh load up the grip. He moved quickly to the bar, vaulting over the side.

The bartender had dropped to the floor when the shooting started. He sat dazed, staring wide-eyed at the dish towel and broken highball glass in his hands.

Bolan grabbed him by the shoulder and the back of his tux, hauled him to his feet and shoved him roughly through the swing door to the kitchen.

The Executioner turned back as the cartel's second wave of attack began. Two men raced through both doors on the highway side of the room. The first, a .45-caliber MAC-10 sputtering in his hands, wore a short-sleeved polo shirt.

Bolan leveled the Desert Eagle on the shirt as his other hand ripped the Beretta from the shoulder rig. Squeezing the trigger of the .44 with his right hand, the Executioner's left thumbed the 93-R selector switch to 3-round burst.

Two mangling Magnum rounds struck the man with the MAC in the breastbone. His mouth opened wide, forming an O of disbelief as he toppled to the tile on the barroom floor.

The Executioner drilled three 9 mm slugs toward the man at the other door. The cartel gunner wisely retreated through the opening.

Bolan dropped below the bar.

The gunman stuck his head around the corner, his dark eyes searching the room.

Bolan stood, the Beretta's second burst nearly severing the head from the man's craning neck.

The warrior leapt over the bar and raced past the falling corpse to the door. Two rounds struck the wall next to his head, and he ducked back inside.

Dropping to the floor, he peered quickly around the corner, his eyes zeroing in on the spot in the trees where he'd hidden the Gonzalezes.

All was quiet in the jungle.

The action was taking place on the beach.

That meant the Gonzalezes hadn't yet been located by the cartel men. For the time being, they were safe where they were.

Bolan wasn't about to lead the killers to them. He raced back across the bar. A cartel gunman stepped through the door from the beach, directly in front of him. The warrior lifted the Desert Eagle, firing point-blank into the surprised face and shouldering the dead man out of the way. He looked up and spotted a beefy gunman just outside. In his black shirt, white tie and sharkskin suit, the man looked like a caricature of the gangster he really was.

But the H&K-94 in the man's hands was no joke.

Bolan let him have it in the throat with a lone round from the Desert Eagle. He glanced down at the H&K-94. The civilian model of the MP-5 he'd left in the jungle, it had a longer, sixteen-inch barrel and fired semiauto only. But that mattered little. The trigger pull was light and short, making the weapon capable of fire almost as rapid as the MP-5 on "rock and roll."

The Executioner scooped it up, jerked two extra 30-round mags from the sharkskin suit, then stepped through the broken glass to the rear of the building.

Pressing his back against the wall, he moved toward the side of the Tortuga Club.

As he neared the corner, the Executioner dropped to the ground once more. Peering low, he saw a single cartel man standing guard with a Winchester pump 12-gauge.

The warrior switched the silenced Beretta to his right hand, stepped around the corner and drilled a 9 mm hollowpoint through the man's heart.

"He's outside!" a voice shouted in Spanish.

The Executioner took off, sprinting from the main building to the first cottage in the long row leading north. At the end of the buildings the sand beach ended and iron shore sprouted from the sea, rising gradually to form a small bluff.

Bolan reached the last cottage. Hidden behind the structure, he looked back to the Tortuga Club Lounge in time to see a dozen armed men enter.

Turning his back once more, the Executioner sprinted across the jagged rock shore and dropped into a small ravine near the bluff.

Temporarily hidden, Bolan set the H&K-94 on a rocky ledge in the bluff. He set both pistols beside the carbine and stripped off his fatigues, reversing them to the camouflage side. In the distance, carried across the incoming tide of the Caribbean, he could still hear the muffled voices of the cartel gunmen.

He dropped the partially spent magazines from both the 93-R and the Desert Eagle and inserted full boxes, making sure a live round rode under the hammer of both weapons. Then, replacing them in their respective holsters, he pulled the camouflage makeup can from his pocket and reapplied the colors to his face and hands. Jamming a fresh clip into the H&K-94, he slung it over his back and began ascending the short rise.

Once at the top, the Executioner took cover behind a large, scraggly boulder. He looked toward the Tortuga Club a hundred and fifty yards to the south.

Armed men stood guard at all four corners of the grounds. Others cautiously made their way in and out of the cottages. Several tourists had been lined up against the walls of their rented bungalows, their hands high in the air, their mouths open wide in shock and terror.

The warrior glanced at the beach. A man wearing a bright red *guayabara* stood holding an assault rifle on the men, women and children who'd been sunbathing and swimming.

The Executioner pulled back around the rock and took a deep breath. He doubted that the cartel men would harm the tourists intentionally. There'd be no gain in it for them. The gunners were just keeping them in line while they searched for him.

But the longer that went on, the greater the possibility that someone might be injured. All it would take would be one well-meaning but untrained would-be hero to lunge for one of the weapons.

A massacre could result.

Bolan opened his map. Another quarter mile north would bring him to Spotter's Bay. From there the coastline curved west. If he could make it past the bay, he could cross the highway unseen and reenter the jungle and get the Gonzalezes out.

He refolded the map, stuffed it into his fatigue shirt and studied the terrain behind him. More iron shore. Rough, jagged. He grinned slightly. The razor-sharp spikes that grew from the shore would tear the cartel men's dress shoes to shreds in no time. They wouldn't do his heavy leather combat boots much good, either, but he'd still be walking long after the drug guards were barefoot.

Bolan turned back to the Tortuga Club and thumbed the safety of the H&K-94 to fire. He leaned forward at the side of the boulder, stretching face-down across the bluff and steadying his arms across the ragged rock.

The H&K-94 had an accuracy range of one hundred yards. The men below were well past that, meaning he'd have to allow for bullet drop. If he was lucky, he'd down a few more gunners before he had to take off across the shore.

But even if he wasn't, the 9 mm carbine would draw the killers' attention away from the innocents.

Sighting down the barrel, Bolan rested the front sight two feet above the head of a cartel man in front of the nearest cottage. The gunner held an Uzi trained on a tourist wearing a swimsuit. Next to the frightened vacationer stood a woman and a little girl.

The Executioner squeezed the trigger and felt the light recoil.

A half second later the cartel gunner with the Uzi fell face forward, blood gushing from the side of his head.

A pudgy Peruvian with a mustache lumbered from the next cottage to the downed man. The man in the red *guayabara* left the beach and raced to join him. Both men knelt briefly next to the dead man. Then the fat gunner struggled to his feet, the Government Model .45 in his hand weaving back and forth across the horizon.

Bolan leveled the barrel a foot and a half above the mustache and sighted through the O-ring.

Another half second later the fat man fell forward into the sand.

A half dozen gunners raced to the scene as the Executioner's third shot sent the man with the red shirt into the growing pile of bodies. A cartel gunman wearing a seersucker vest and matching slacks pointed toward the bluff, and the other heads turned toward Bolan.

He rose to his feet and extended the H&K-94 to arm's length over his head. A moment passed as the men around the bodies stood frozen, staring up at him.

Bolan dropped the assault rifle back to his side and raised his other hand. A hard smile curled his lips as he waved to the gunmen below.

BOLAN FELT the sharp rocks stabbing against the hard rubber soles of his boots as he crossed the iron shore. He heard a shot, then the air buzzed as the round flew past his ear.

He twisted as he ran, sending four rapid-fire semiauto 9 mm rounds flying back in the direction of his pursuers.

The warrior rounded the northeast point of the island and cut back inland, out of sight. He saw the small inlet of Spotter's Bay in the distance and jogged cautiously back toward the highway.

Taking cover behind a deserted shack in the wilderness, Bolan studied the road. No longer paved, the dirt-and-gravel throughway still continued along the north side of the island. Across the road he faced another low grassland before he'd reach the cover of thicker growth again.

There was no time like the present, the Executioner thought as he sprinted into the open.

Making it without incident to the jungle, the warrior stayed close to the edge of the clearing—far enough in to be invisible, yet far enough back that he could retain surveillance of the road. He followed the curvature of the woodland until the paved highway began once more. Several cartel vehicles patrolled the strip of asphalt as he continued toward where he'd left the Gonzalezes.

The Executioner wondered about Reuben and Tana as he chopped his way through the foliage with the ATC. They had to have heard the gunfire at the Tortuga Club. Their first instinct would have been to flee. If they'd followed that instinct, they could be dead already.

The interior literally crawled with other cartel search parties. Reuben was armed, smart and trained, but he'd be no match for them in his condition.

As the Tortuga Club became visible in the distance, Bolan saw two dozen armed men standing in the parking lot. Suddenly a car squealed to a stop next to them. The driver rolled down his window as a gunner with an automatic pistol in his hand walked forward.

The man leaned into the car. A split second later he shoved the pistol in his waistband, turned to the others and shouted.

The gunners headed for their vehicles.

Bolan reached the cocoon as the cars sped off, back toward the west end of the island. He slowed his pace, moving quietly toward the camouflage shelter. When he was three feet away, he dropped to the ground. "Reuben," he whispered.

No response.

Bolan crawled forward. At the edge of the cocoon, he repeated, "Reuben?"

Silence.

The Executioner reached slowly forward, digging a break through the leaves and vines with his hand. He peered inside and found himself looking down the barrel of the Valmet M-78.

Reuben saw him, rose painfully from the ground and whispered, "Is it clear?"

"For now. But we've got to get moving."

The Executioner tore through the wall of the shelter as Tana got to her feet. Around the edges of the cammo makeup on her face, her skin had turned a pallid white.

"We thought you were dead," she whispered.

Bolan smiled down at her. "Not yet."

Shrill sirens screamed to the south. Then the screeching sounds came from the east as police cars rounded the coast and pulled up at the Tortuga Club.

Moving quickly to the edge of the trees, the Executioner watched as six unarmed officers, wearing bright red slacks, white tunics and pith helmets, leapt from the vehicles.

Two of the men carried nightsticks.

Bolan shook his head. They were lucky the cartel hitters had opted to leave.

He draped the MP-5, H&K-94 and the Valmet over his shoulders, leaving Reuben with his SIG-Sauer and the lighter MAC-10. With the Gonzalezes in tow, he charted a southwest course across the interior of Grand Cayman, recrossing some of the same jungles and swampland they'd traversed earlier in the day.

Bolan pulled out the map. If they followed the road to their right, they'd emerge from the jungle on the north side of the island at Old Man Bay. A long way from the airport.

Grimaldi would have to navigate them through the countless cartel vehicles that now patrolled the roads.

To their left the road led south, intersecting finally with the main highway that circled the island, near Frank Sound.

Bolan frowned, studying the map. Farther southwest, past the villages of Bodden Town, the road cut away from the sea. Several other small hamlets appeared along the shore. The Executioner's eyes fell on the tiny burg of Savannah. It was several miles out of their way, but would seem an unlikely spot for them to emerge.

And they'd be only a few minutes from the airport when he phoned Grimaldi again.

Bolan folded the map back into his pocket and turned back to the highway. He waited for an ancient Chevy pickup to pass, then led Reuben and Tana to the road. He watched Reuben as they crossed the steaming asphalt. The DEA man walked better now. The pain in his hip seemed to be working itself out as he went.

But the man still stumbled occasionally, and without his wife holding his elbow, Bolan suspected that his progress would be even more difficult.

The Executioner helped them both over a short barbed-wire fence, and they reentered the jungle.

He'd chopped and hacked through the trees for fifteen minutes when he heard the voices. The warrior froze where he stood, holding a hand up behind him to halt Reuben and Tana. Somewhere in the distance the heavy sound of boots thrashing through the undergrowth carried through the leaves.

Dropping silently to the jungle floor, the Executioner motioned the Gonzalezes to do the same.

"Aye, man," said an unseen voice from somewhere in front of them. "Captain, can we rest a moment now?"

"Aye, Sergeant Ebanks," another voice answered. "Make sure you don't shoot yourself in the foot with your new pistol when you sit."

More voices laughed.

Bolan rolled to his side, facing Reuben and Tana. He held a finger to his lips, pointed to both of them in turn, then held up both hands, palm out.

The Gonzalezes nodded.

The warrior crawled slowly forward through the vines, noiselessly making his way toward the voices. Cigarette smoke drifted through the foliage to his nostrils.

When he had gone fifteen yards, a spot of scarlet flashed through the green undergrowth. Bolan moved closer and saw the blue-striped, crimson uniform trousers of the Cayman Island police.

In the center of a small marsh sat seven officers. Dressed in ineffective combinations of camouflage gear and their usual uniforms, they'd taken seats on several logs rotting in the mud. Several of them played with the guns they held, racking the slides of automatic pistols and spinning the cylinders of revolvers like young boys who'd just opened their presents on Christmas morning.

Six of the men sat together on the trunk that had been dragged to the center of the clearing. The other sat alone across the clearing, near the edge of the trees, facing Bolan. He wore his stark white uniform tunic above a pair of O.D. green fatigue pants.

As Bolan watched, he called to the others. "I think, Captain McTaggert," he said, twirling a stainless-steel Smith & Wesson Model 66 on the end of his trigger finger, "that when this is over, I'll fly to Texas and become a cowboy-sheriff."

The men burst into laughter once more.

Bolan crawled backward, retracing his steps toward Reuben and Tana. These men had obviously been sent to search for the plane shortly after the crash. They'd been armed and probably told there *might* be some threat from the outside.

But they had no idea what had happened at the Tortuga Club. If they had, they wouldn't be laughing.

And so far, they'd been lucky. They hadn't encountered any of the cartel search parties.

If they had, they'd be dead.

Bolan led Reuben and Tana back along the trail, away from the police officers. When they'd covered fifty yards, they turned north, making their way quietly around the search party.

When he was satisfied that they were out of earshot, Bolan stopped. He hesitated to go back. But these inexperienced men would be sitting ducks if they continued with the attitude they now had.

Somehow he had to warn them that their tiny island had been invaded by an army of killers—men who not only wielded more firepower, but very well might outnumber their force, as well.

Leaving Tana and Reuben to rest, the Executioner crawled back to the clearing. He approached slowly, peering through the leaves to see that the men in the center of the clearing still faced away from him. Their voices were low, and one of the men, wearing a red beret, had fallen asleep.

The man with the Model 66 still sat near the edge of the jungle. He'd produced a paperback novel from somewhere and sat quietly reading.

The Executioner reached out of the vines, cupping a big hand around the man's mouth and jerking him back into the trees.

Bolan pressed the barrel of the Desert Eagle against the officer's temple and whispered softly into his ear. "I'm going to let go of you now. Make a sound, and I'll kill you. Understand?"

The man nodded vigorously.

Bolan removed his hand. "Turn around."

He leaned in, resting the weapon on the bridge of the officer's nose. "You don't have any idea what's happening," he whispered, "but I'll summarize for you. You've heard of the Lima cartel?"

The man nodded, still staring at the barrel of the Desert Eagle.

"They've sent killers from Peru to look for a DEA agent who survived the crash, a DEA agent who can finger some of their bosses and destroy their operation. I think you get the picture." The Executioner paused, and the terrified cop's head bobbed again. "They'll kill every one of you, too, if they find you out here. You're no match for them. Get the hell out of the jungle. Now. You understand?"

Another nod.

"Good. Now, turn back around."

As the petrified cop slowly turned, the Executioner shoved the Desert Eagle into his belt. Reaching up, he encircled the man's throat with one arm and pressed the other into the back of his neck. Pushing and pulling, the warrior jammed his wrist into the man's windpipe, cutting off the oxygen to his brain.

The Cayman cop struggled briefly, then went limp. Bolan lowered him to the ground. By the time the cop came to, he and the Gonzalezes would be far away.

And then, if the Cayman Island officers had any sense at all, they'd make their own escape from the predators who hunted this jungle.

4

Jack Grimaldi yanked the visor of the Alaskan bush pilot's hat down over his eyes against the sun. He pulled the rented Ford LTD from the airport parking lot onto the blacktop leading to the highway.

Reaching the intersection, Stony Man Farm's ace pilot saw the sign announcing George Town to his right. To his left the road led along the southern coast of the island, through Savannah, Bodden Town and Breakers, to the tiny village of East End and then upward to the Tortuga Club near the northeast corner of the island.

And Striker.

Grimaldi glanced down to the speedometer, making sure he was still under the posted limit. There was no hurry. Everything had gone smoothly so far. For once maybe one of Striker's missions would be routine.

Grimaldi was nearing Half Moon Bay when he heard the shrill sirens behind him. Glancing into the rearview mirror, he saw two blue-and-white police cars bearing down on him. The pilot slowed the Ford and pulled to the side of the road. The cars raced past.

A traffic accident? Maybe.

The pilot drove on, tense. He ordered himself to relax. There were a million and one reasons why the police might be heading hell-bent for leather toward the same end of the island as he.

Grimaldi passed through East End and followed the highway north, seeing a rusting ship reefed a few hundred yards from the shore. As he passed a tall radio tower, several cars drove slowly toward him.

The first car passed, loaded with hard-looking, dark-skinned men. The second car carried a similar cargo.

The Stony Man pilot kept his eyes on the road, watching the strange procession out of the corner of his eye as a third, fourth and fifth car passed. As he drove past to the last car in line, a glint of fading sunlight reflected off the barrel of a rifle, just above window level.

He forced himself to stay at the speed limit. Whatever had happened was over. Striker was either alive or dead. If Bolan had finally given his life in his war everlasting, then there was nothing he could do.

But if he hadn't, and he and the Gonzalezes were on the run again, they'd need his assistance. He wouldn't be any help if he got detained by the local cops.

Grimaldi rounded a small curve in the road and saw the Tortuga Club in the distance. As he neared, the outlines of bodies littering the parking lot came into focus.

Striker's might well be among them. But if it was, the big guy had damn sure taken a bunch of the cartel players with him.

Grimaldi slowed, then came to a complete stop as a tall, black police officer stepped from the parking lot onto the highway.

The cop raised his hand, then leaned down, the fading sunlight sparkling off the silver badge pinned to his white tunic. Matching captain's bars gleamed on his shoulders. Above the pouch pocket on the other side of his chest was a name tag—Elvis Bodden.

Captain Bodden rested a stout forearm on the driver's window of the Ford, frowning.

"You're American?" the man asked.

"Yes." Grimaldi started to reach for his wallet, intending to produce the temporary driver's permit he'd purchased when he rented the car.

The big man's hand shot to Grimaldi's wrist. "Slowly," he ordered.

Grimaldi pulled the permit from his wallet and held it up.

Bodden looked nervously over his shoulder, as if unconvinced that whatever had happened at the Tortuga Club was over. Turning back, he studied Grimaldi's permit. "Where are you staying, Mr. Wolfe?"

"Seven Mile Beach. Uh, the Coral Caymanian."

Bodden continued to stare at him. "Why are you here?"

"Well, I don't know. Just looking around." He pointed to the small Instamatic camera on the passenger's seat. "Heard there were some wrecked ships and stuff on the reef at this end. I—"

The big cop straightened. "We're conducting an investigation, Mr. Wolfe. You will drive forward to the first driveway, turn around and return to George Town. Immediately.''

''But Officer, I wanted to—''

Bodden raised his right foot high in the air, then brought it down hard, stamping the pavement. *''Immediately.''*

Grimaldi nodded. Slowly he drove past the carnage in the parking lot. Through the open doors of the club, he could see more bodies lying inside. Reaching the driveway Bodden had indicated, he pulled in, then glanced into his side mirror.

The burly cop had stopped another car on the highway.

Grimaldi threw the Ford into Park and slid from behind the wheel. He walked quickly into the bar where several other uniformed men stood staring down at the bodies on the tile. One of them looked up as he entered.

''Uh, sorry,'' Grimaldi said. ''Guess you're not open right now.'' He returned to the Ford.

The pilot backed out of the drive and turned onto the highway. The captain held his hand high in the air again as he neared. A surly scowl covered his face.

''Mr. Wolfe, why did you enter the club?'' he demanded.

The pilot shrugged. ''Just curious. I didn't know what had happened.''

Bodden stuck his thick neck through the window, his face an inch from Grimaldi's. ''You'll return without further incident,'' he ordered, ''or you'll be arrested for interfering with our investigation.''

Grimaldi tapped the foot feed and started back along the highway. He passed through East End again and followed the coast back to Breakers.

He thought back to the brawny cop at the Tortuga Club. He hadn't lied to Bodden. He *didn't* know exactly what had happened back at the resort.

But what he did know was that Striker, and Reuben and Tana Gonzalez weren't among the dead littering the ground. He pressed down on the gas pedal and roared back in the direction of the airport.

They were alive, somewhere in the jungle, and they'd emerge again soon.

And when they did, Jack Grimaldi intended to be there to help them.

DARKNESS FELL QUICKLY over the jungle. The full, round moon had risen high in the sky as Bolan and the Gonzalezes reached the narrow blacktop leading to Newlands. Staying just inside the tree line, the Executioner led them south until the main highway became visible near the small village of Savannah.

Leaving Reuben and Tana to wait in the darkness, the warrior moved cautiously to the edge of the trees that ran along the side of the highway. Several scattered houses sat haphazardly along the road on the other side. At the intersection of the highway and the Newlands blacktop, the Executioner could see an elderly man locking the rusty red gasoline tank in front of a small grocery store. The old man wore a ragged mesh baseball cap above his sparse gray beard. As Bolan watched, he killed the lights within the building, walked to a battered Toyota pickup and drove south, disappearing into the darkness along the blacktop.

Bolan scanned the village. Through the open windows of the tiny houses, he saw lights, images dancing across television screens, movement. But no one appeared on the streets.

By now Grimaldi would have figured out what happened at the Tortuga Club and returned to the airport to await further instructions. It should be a simple enough matter to break into the small store and call him.

The Executioner squinted into the darkness, his eyes searching for telephone lines. That plan had only one drawback—the store didn't have a phone.

Under the lone streetlight at the intersection, Bolan saw the sign: Pedro Castle—Restaurant And Bar—½ Mile. Rows of carefully planted cedars led past the sign into the darkness.

Returning to Reuben and Tana, Bolan helped them to their feet. "We'll cross the highway here," he said. "Keep to the trees and keep quiet. There's a place called Pedro Castle a half mile up that's bound to have a phone."

Reuben and Tana nodded.

He took one of Reuben's arms; Tana took the other. They waited as a Volkswagen van slowed through town, then sprinted across the street and darted behind the row of trees leading toward the castle.

Bolan studied Reuben as they crept through the cedars. The stress, both mental and physical, was beginning to take its toll on the man. Earlier in the afternoon he'd seemed to snap out of it, and the warrior had had a fleeting moment of hope that he'd been wrong about the extent of the man's head injury.

But as evening had approached, the tough little agent had slowed again, losing his footing on a regular basis. The Executioner realized now that adrenaline had been fueling Reuben Gonzalez earlier.

Bolan glanced at him, panting as he limped along, his head hanging low on his chest.

That adrenaline tank was almost empty.

They kept to the trees, making their way slowly toward the south shore. After fifteen minutes they saw the lights of the castle through the branches. The soft sounds of calypso music drifted toward them.

Leaving them hidden, Bolan moved to the edge of the trees. The ancient stone castle was three stories high, the first and second floors enclosed in modern wood siding. The faded stone of the third floor peeked through at the top like a ghost emerging from the past.

A small walkway led to the building's main entrance. A green-and-white-striped canvas canopy covered the final approach to wide double doors leading into the dining room.

The Executioner crept along the tree line, angling away from the castle toward the sea. As he passed the corner of the building, he saw a large patio and the source of the calypso music. To one side a quartet of conga drums, two guitars and flute played softly under the stars. Several diners sat eating their dinners.

At the edge of the patio near the parking lot was the gray-haired man from the Savannah gas station. He upended a bottle of Red Stripe beer, then added it to the growing mass of dead soldiers on the table before him.

A sharp hiss sounded from the sea. Bolan turned toward the craggy iron shore on his right and saw water shoot high into the air.

He stepped from the trees into the shadows along the shore. A small ridge dropped a few feet from the jagged ledge into the water, forming a rock-enclosed pool. The water hissed and blasted up again as the tide shot into the "blowhole" through some hidden crevice below the surface.

Bolan moved along the rock, watching the patio. An open door led into the castle's bar. Several old men sat at the scarred wooden counter, and at the far end was an ancient black rotary phone.

Moving back through the shadows, the Executioner returned to find Reuben asleep again. He roused the groggy man to consciousness and helped him to his feet.

Bolan dropped both H&Ks, the MAC and the Valmet to the ground. He'd have his hands full with the DEA man. They'd have to return after calling Grimaldi and pick them up.

Bolan and Tana helped Reuben through the trees to the iron shore and lowered him to the rocks next to the blowhole. The warrior rolled his fatigue jacket into a pillow for the man's head, then turned to Tana. "I need your help again."

Tana looked up, her face a veil of open, innocent trust.

"There's a phone inside the bar," Bolan continued. "There's a good chance the cartel's got a man inside, and there's an equally good chance it's someone who saw me at the Tortuga Club.'' He frowned. He was about to ask a lot of her, and he wasn't sure she was up to it.

Bolan took a deep breath. ''I'm going to give you the number of the airport, Mrs. Gonzalez. I'll watch you the entire time.''

Slowly Tana nodded.

He reached into his buttpack and produced a small notepad and pen. Scribbling across a page, he tore it from the pad and handed it to her. ''Here's the number. Have them page Bob Wolfe. We don't know who's in the bar, so just say hello when he answers and tell him you're at Pedro Castle. He'll figure out the rest. Do you understand all that?'' Bolan paused, waiting for her reaction.

The fear on Tana's face faded. ''Yes.''

''Any questions, Mrs. Gonzalez?''

''Yes.'' She paused, a nervous smile crossing her face in the semidarkness. ''Would you please start calling me Tana? Mrs. Gonzalez makes me feel so...old.''

Bolan chuckled. The woman had finally come around. She was out of shock. ''Okay, Tana.''

Tana squatted next to the blowhole. Leaning down, she washed the camouflage makeup from her face. She stood, then leaned down again and kissed her sleeping husband lightly on the lips.

She turned to Bolan again. ''He'll be all right, won't he?''

Bolan nodded. "He's tough, and he'll hang on. We'll get him to a doctor just as soon as we're clear of all this."

Tana didn't answer as she retied the shirt around her waist. Bolan helped her up and over the edge of the rocks.

Looking briefly back, she started toward the castle.

Bolan drew the Beretta from shoulder leather. He rested his forearms on the rock, watching as Tana stepped out of the shadows and into the overhead lights of the castle's courtyard. The little woman looked like any other vacationer as she crossed through the diners on the patio and entered the door to the bar.

Through the door Bolan saw her speak briefly to the bartender, who pointed toward the phone in the corner.

Tana lifted the receiver and dialed. Bolan saw her lips move then stop as she waited for Grimaldi to answer the page.

The Executioner grinned in the darkness as she spoke again a few seconds later. The Stony Man pilot couldn't have been more than a few feet away from the phone.

As Tana replaced the receiver in the cradle, Bolan heard the sound of car engines approaching along the blacktop from the highway. He glanced toward the noise as two cars pulled into the parking lot.

In the bright overhead lights of the lot, the Executioner saw eight men exit the vehicles and stand next to the cars.

None of the men had guns. At least not in their hands. But the telltale bulges under their jackets and shirts left little doubt as to their identity.

Bolan glanced back at Tana. She stood in the doorway, talking to the bartender again. The Executioner leaned forward, trying to will her to move, to get the hell out of there and back to the shore before the inevitable happened.

One of the men from the cars, wearing a white cotton dress shirt and matching slacks, walked across the lot, stopping at the table where the bearded gas station attendant sat. He reached into his pocket, dropped several coins on the table and spoke briefly.

Bolan saw the old man nod and point toward the bar.

The Executioner glanced behind him. Reuben was still asleep.

The man in white returned to the cars. A moment later the remaining seven men followed him back across the lot toward the patio.

Bolan turned back to the door as Tana stepped onto the patio, a bright smile covering her face.

As he rose from cover and vaulted up onto the ridge, he saw the first of the cartel gunners point toward her and draw his gun.

MARINO MARIATEGUI HEARD the change in the engine's drone as the Piper Cub began its descent. Mariategui stared through the windshield at the bright runway lights in the distance. He straightened the lapel of his white silk suit with one hand while the fingers of the other absentmindedly traced the scar on his face.

He thought back to the many times he'd been to Grand Cayman in the past. For years he'd combined business with pleasure, flying to the island to deposit money into the Lima cartel's anonymously numbered bank accounts, then recuperating from the stress of his profession on the sands of Seven Mile Beach.

The wheels touched down on the landing strip, and the pilot braked the Piper Cub to a halt. A customs official wearing navy blue slacks, a white shirt and a blue tie bearing the islands' Sir Turtle logo walked forward, a clipboard in his hand.

"Ah, Mr. Mariategui," he said as the cartel man stepped down from the plane. "It's good to see you again."

"Thank you, Benjamin."

"Your office phoned earlier, asking us to pass you through quickly." He reached into his shirt pocket and produced a tiny stub of white chalk. Leaning forward, he drew a quick X on Mariategui's briefcase. "I'll escort you."

Mariategui followed the customs official into the airport terminal. They stopped briefly at the passport window while the man called Benjamin reached up, taking the stamp from the woman in the booth.

Mariategui felt his stomach begin to burn. He popped two antacid tablets into his mouth as he waited for the official to stamp his passport.

The cartel underboss's silk suit clung wetly to his skin as they crossed to the other side of the terminal. Benjamin opened the door to the parking lot, then waited while Mariategui fished inside his sticky jacket, coming up with a sealed white envelope.

The customs man's face scanned nervously across the terminal for curious eyes, then the envelope disappeared inside his shirt.

"Have a nice stay, Mr. Mariategui. And don't hesitate to call me if I can be of further assistance."

A long, cream-colored sedan pulled to a stop in front of Mariategui. A short man with curly black hair jumped from the vehicle and opened the right rear door. Mariategui slid into the back seat, thankful for the air conditioner the driver had left running.

As they pulled away from the airport toward George Town, Mariategui slipped out of his jacket and folded it neatly on the seat next to him. "Fill me in on the latest developments, Alberto."

The driver reached for a pair of sunglasses clipped to the visor above him. Wrapping them around his face, he said, "Cha-cha has received some type of assistance from the U.S." He paused, taking a deep breath.

"What are you talking about?" he said. "That's impossible. We've taken care of that."

"Yes," Alberto said. "Our government official here was successful in convincing the rest of the Caymanian Parliament that they needed no U.S. intervention. But *someone* has come to Pasquela's...Gonzalez's aid anyway. We don't know who he is, but he's real good at what he does."

"Explain."

Alberto shifted uncomfortably behind the wheel, and Mariategui could see he dreaded delivering bad news.

Alberto finally spoke. "Several of our men in the jungle saw someone parachute onto the island. Later two search parties were discovered—dead. There was evidence that they'd found Cha-cha and his wife, and this mysterious American had rescued them before they could be executed. Later the man was spotted at a resort on the east coast of the island—"

"The Tortuga Club?" Mariategui broke in. "I know it well. I have stayed there several times."

"Yes. I believe that was the name."

"So?"

"We believe he entered the club to call for more assistance. Our men attacked."

"They killed him?"

Alberto paused again. "No," he said hesitantly. "He killed them."

Mariategui sat back against the seat, his hand fingering the scar on his cheek. "Where are the rest of the men now?"

"Most are patrolling the island's highway and other roads. Cha-cha and the American will have to come out of the jungle eventually."

"And the search parties within the interior?"

Alberto flinched. "Many of the men have come out of the jungle, Mr. Mariategui. They refuse to return." Alberto paused. "They believe the American is a spirit. They are calling him the White Ghost."

Mariategui felt the anger race through his veins. He reached into the side pocket of his coat, found the package of antacid tablets and popped two into his mouth.

The sedan passed through George Town and started up the highway leading north along Seven Mile Beach. Mariategui watched through the windows as men, women and children strolled along the roadside in front of the various hotels.

As they rode in silence, the Lima cartel boss reached into his briefcase and withdrew a nickel-plated Colt Government Model 9 mm automatic. He set it on the seat beside him, then sat back again to ponder the situation.

Many of the men already on the island were Indian, from the various tribes in the Andes. The superstitions of their fathers were never far from their conscious minds. The same applied to the fresh men who now waited off the north coast of the island on what Cayman officials thought was a cargo ship.

The men on the ship knew nothing of the massacre of their comrades in the jungle and at the Tortuga Club. But as soon as they joined the gunmen on the island, the stories would sweep through the troops. This White Ghost legend would provoke their backward imaginations, rendering them as frightened and useless as the men who'd fled the jungle.

Mariategui lifted the Colt and slid it into the waistband of his silk slacks. He'd have to do something about this ridiculous story, end it quickly before it sabotaged all of his efforts.

Alberto broke the silence. "Whoever this man is, he escaped back into the jungle. We believe Cha-cha and his wife are still with him."

Mariategui watched the driver in the rearview mirror. "Do you believe he's a spirit, Alberto?"

Alberto hesitated, then said, "Of course not, boss."

"Then he must be a man, Alberto," Mariategui continued. "Over forty men have already been sent to the island. You're telling me that they're no match for this one man? One man who must also take care of a helpless woman and Cha-cha, who is reported to be severely injured?"

Alberto didn't answer.

Mariategui sat back against the seat and stared out the window as they entered the northern village of West Bay. The highway ended near the old town hall, and Alberto cut onto a side street, then took a small road leading out of town to Spanish Bay on the north shore.

When they reached the sea, Mariategui stepped from the vehicle. A quarter mile offshore he saw the lights of the large freighter anchored on the other side of the coral reef.

A crumbling stone staircase led from the highway to a small pier. Mariategui saw the waiting speedboat. A cartel man he vaguely recognized from Lima sat waiting behind the wheel.

Descending the steps, Mariategui stepped into the boat. Neither he nor the driver spoke as they splashed over the reef to the freighter. When they arrived, the cartel underboss grasped the ladder attached to the side of the ship and hauled himself on board. He was greeted by the captain.

"Where are the men, Manuel?" Mariategui asked as his feet hit the deck.

"I've kept them out of sight below, boss," the man in the skipper's cap answered nervously. "They're in the hold, awaiting your orders."

Mariategui nodded. He followed Manuel across the deck to the ladder leading down into the bowels of the ship.

Below, the underboss found seventy men dressed in camouflage fatigues, pressed tightly into the hold. They sat on crates, boxes, the floor, and stood uncomfortably in every nook and cranny the ship afforded. The mass of flesh pressed farther back as he descended the ladder.

The men suddenly quieted as Mariategui turned to face them. Scattered within the throng were a dozen or so who were dressed in ripped slacks and soiled dress shirts.

Mariategui felt his eyes narrow. So. Some of the men already here had boarded the ship. This White Ghost nonsense would already be circulating, contaminating the troops. He'd have to act fast, decisively.

One of the men, tall and wearing a neatly trimmed beard, stepped forward. "We're ready to issue arms, Mr. Mariategui," he said hesitantly.

Mariategui nodded. He lifted a crowbar from a nearby crate and pried the lid off the box. From inside he lifted an M-16A2 assault rifle, still wrapped in oil-soaked wax paper.

Moving to another of the crates, he popped the lid to find 20-round magazines for the weapons. A third wooden container yielded stacked boxes of Remington .223 soft-point ammunition.

Nervous whispers and an occasional anxious laugh punctuated the silence as Mariategui handed the crowbar to the man with the beard. He watched while the man popped the lids on the remaining crates.

Mariategui wondered briefly who the Americans had sent to rescue Cha-cha. Whoever he was, this White Ghost, he'd succeeded in terrifying the Lima cartel's top gunmen.

The underboss waited silently while the ordnance was issued, then leaned back against an open crate and called the men to order. "You're about to embark on a mission that may well affect the rest of your lives."

A man wearing a brush-scratched leather shoulder holster over his shredded shirt spoke from the back of the room. "Mr. Mariategui," he said in a frightened voice, "the Americans have sent a demon to protect the traitor."

Hushed murmurs of support flew through the room. Then a short, wiry man who squatted at the front of the group said, "He is like Satan himself. He can't die."

Mariategui looked down at the ferret-faced man. "Oswaldo," he said. "When you were hired two years ago, your family was starving while you labored like an animal in the coffee fields of Brazil. Do you remember?"

The small man's black eyes dropped to the floor. He nodded.

Mariategui looked up to the tall man at the back of the room who had spoken earlier. "And you, José. You were a small-time pickpocket and purse snatcher when Hector Pizarro found a place for you within the organization. Now you live in a fine house. You eat the finest food available on the face of the earth. And you drink the finest wines with that food. Need I remind you who is responsible for this change in your life-style?''

He didn't wait for an answer. His eyes flew across the faces of the men. ''You're superstitious cowards. We're facing men.'' The underboss paused, taking in a deep breath. Then he let his voice rise an octave and screamed, *''Men!* Not spirits! Not ghosts!''

Mariategui's gaze fell to the floor, and he shook his head in disgust. He spoke more quietly when he said, ''And a woman. But perhaps that's fitting. You're acting like women yourselves.''

He waited as the men's fearful expressions changed to shame. Good. He'd attacked their masculinity, their macho pride, and it was having the desired result.

After a few moments he continued in a softer voice. ''If Reuben Gonzalez is allowed to reach the United States, indictments against many of our affiliates, including myself, will mean the end for you and your families.''

Mariategui looked up, picking out a man near the center of the group. ''You were a police officer before you came to me, Franco. Why did you wish to go to work for Hector Pizarro?''

The man, graying around the temples, looked down at the floor.

Mariategui nodded. ''I'll tell you why. Because even with the graft we paid you to look the other way, you knew you could do better if you joined us. Do you wish to return to the life of a cop?''

The cartel underboss smiled. He let his gaze fall to another man near the front. "Life has been cruel to you, Paco. Although it wasn't your fault, you were suited for nothing but the most menial labor. If Chacha lives, you'll return to the barrio where I found you. And once again your wife and daughters will be whores, turning tricks so that they may eat." He watched as Paco's face reddened in shame.

Mariategui scanned the group. Good. They were broken.

It was time to rebuild.

Mariategui addressed the men as a whole once more. "You're all good men," he said, "and I'll not lie to you. You're facing a man who's a specialist at what he does." The cartel man allowed his voice to rise slightly again, taking on the zeal of the Christian missionaries he'd heard as a small child. "But he's a man, not a ghost. And you're specialists, as well. You've received the finest training available. Each and every one of you is a match for this man. Together you can't fail."

Mariategui heard more murmurs throughout the room as his words bred courage among the troops. He felt an electric current race through the atmosphere as the men's adrenal glands activated and joined force to create a giant tidal wave of energy.

"Will we allow Cha-cha and this other man to take what we have worked for?" Mariategui shouted.

"No!" the men cried in unison, their angry voices echoing through the hold.

"Then what will we do?"

"Kill him!" came the furious response.

The cartel man let his voice drop again. He looked down to the floor. "I'll order no man to fight. Anyone who doesn't wish to leave the ship may remain. When we return to Lima, he will be paid, then released from employment."

Mariategui rose from his seat and turned toward the door. Then, turning back to the men, he said, "Who's with me?"

As if of one mind, close to a hundred men raised their rifles into the air. "We're with you until death!"

Mariategui led the way up the ladder to the deck. He watched as the near-delirious men inflated rubber dinghies and began paddling wildly toward the island.

When the last dingy had left, he dropped back down into the speedboat. He watched the foolish men in the rubber craft as the driver raced past them across the reef.

Most of them had been peasants before coming to work for the Lima cartel. He'd trained many of them himself, using the knowledge he'd gained as a gunman for the Medellín cartel so many years before. Each *was* good at what he did, and each *did* live a far better life than he had before joining Pizarro's organization.

As the driver tied the speedboat to the dock once more, the cartel underboss stepped away from the boat and glanced back at the oncoming dinghies. He wondered briefly which of them wouldn't return to Peru.

And he realized, his heart devoid of emotion, that he didn't care.

5

Tana Gonzalez tried to concentrate on the calypso music as she crossed the patio. Goose bumps broke out on her arms and shoulders as she entered the bar. Her eyes fell on the phone at the corner of the wooden counter.

She lifted the receiver to her ear and dialed the number Belasko had given her. A few seconds later she heard, "Owen Roberts International Airport, how may I help you?"

"Uh, Mr. Bob Wolfe," she said.

"Yes?"

"Uh, could you page him, please?"

"Certainly. One moment."

As she waited, Tana surveyed the old men at the bar. In their dirty fishing caps and frayed shirts, none of them looked like killers. But what did a killer look like? she wondered. Until today, the only violent death she'd ever witnessed was on TV and at the movies. The good guys always won, and even the bad guys who got killed showed up next week in another series.

This was different. This was real.

Tana felt herself shudder as an old man in a soiled sailor's cap glanced toward her. He took a sip of beer, then smiled, his broken yellow teeth showing brown around the gums.

She turned away, her eyes falling on a discarded brochure advertising Pedro Castle.

The Castle is now used as an Inn, she read silently, trying to calm her nerves. *With guest rooms located on the second and third floors. Restaurant and bar in the very room where Blackbeard the Pirate and his cutthroats once gathered after plundering....*

Tana quit reading. It might be mere legend. Even if it was true, that had been three hundred years ago.

But the cutthroats plundering the island tonight were far too real.

She stared out through the open door, toward the sea. Was Belasko still watching? Yes. He would be. Somehow that thought relaxed her. Reuben had been right. If anyone could get them out of here and to safety, it would be this man.

Tana heard the line click, and then a voice said, "Yes?"

"Er, Mr. Wolfe?"

"Yes."

She looked around the bar again. None of the old men were paying her any attention. "Uh, do you know who this is?" she whispered into the phone.

"Yes. Why are *you* calling. Is...your new friend all right?"

"Yes, yes," she said quickly. "He's waiting. We're all waiting."

"Where are you?"

"We're at..." She felt the fear flow through her chest. Where were they? She'd forgotten the name. Oh, dear God, what if she couldn't remember?

"Where are you?" the voice repeated. "I'll come get you."

"I...I can't remember." Tana was almost in tears. "It's out in the country somewhere. It's a castle..." Her eyes returned frantically to the brochure. "Pedro Castle."

"Pedro Castle?" the man repeated.

"Yes. That's it."

"I'm on my way," the voice told her. She heard another click as the line went dead.

Tana dropped the phone back on the hook and turned toward the door.

The bartender leaned forward, setting his dish towel on the counter in front of her. "Get you something, miss?" he asked.

"No...no, thank you."

He frowned, eyeing her up and down. "You all right, miss?"

"Yes."

"What you drinking?" he asked. "Have one on the house. Whatever you been through, you look like you could use it."

"No, really..." She started for the door.

"Piña colada?" the man asked. "How's about a nice rum punch? It's on me."

Tana ignored him and stepped out onto the patio. The band had picked up the pace, going into more lively music as most of the diners finished their dinners.

She squinted through the darkness, trying to make out the ghostly shadow that seemed to rise from the very sea itself. Then she recognized Belasko's tall form as he walked quickly toward the patio.

In his hand was one of his big pistols.

Tana stopped dead as he raised the gun and pointed it somewhere to her right. She turned to see several cruel-looking men step from the parking lot to the patio.

The lead man had a thick, bushy mustache, looking like a Mexican bandit. He reached under his shirt and pulled out a gun.

Tana suddenly felt weak, light-headed. The blood in her head seemed to flow down her body, through her legs and out her feet. She felt her knees buckle under her as a soft *pffft* came from Belasko's direction.

As she fell to the patio floor, she saw bright red blood fly from the side of the mustachioed man's head.

And all hell broke loose.

Gunshots seemed to boom from all sides. She hugged the concrete as the restaurant guests dived to the ground around her.

Tana tried to crawl farther under the table. Suddenly strong hands gripped her waist from behind. She felt like a rag doll as she was lifted off the ground. Before she could scream, the hands released her and she went flying through the door back into the bar.

A split second later Bolan came hurtling in behind her.

Tana watched in awe as the big man leaned back through the door and shot his gun. He ducked back as shots boomed and chips of rotting wood flew from the door frame around him.

He leaned down, hauling her from the floor with one hand and dragging her through a door leading to the dining room.

A half dozen diners lay on the floor in the corner, away from the windows. Through the window Tana could see the lighted parking lot. The men with the guns had taken cover behind their cars.

Bolan dropped her in the corner next to an open door. She glanced through the opening and saw the stairs leading up into the castle.

The big man moved to the window. Sticking his gun back in its holster, he pulled the other one, even bigger, from under his jacket.

Tana thought her eardrums had exploded as he fired through the window. The glass shattered and one of the men outside fell to the ground.

Bolan dropped below the window as bullets sailed through the opening, crashing into the walls above Tana's head and sending white dust raining down over her and the other people huddled in the corner.

He stood again, shooting, and another of the men dropped to the ground.

Gunshots blasted from the patio. Through the window, Tana saw the men turn in that direction and return fire. The big man rose and fired, hitting two more gunners while their attention was diverted.

A split second later Reuben staggered through the door to the dining room. He had his pistol in his hand.

It fell to the end of his arm as he dropped exhausted to the floor, gasping for air.

Tana crawled across the carpet to her husband as more shots whizzed above her head. Reuben looked up at her as she leaned over him. "Are you...shot?" she asked, not sure she wanted to hear the answer.

Reuben shook his head, slowly rising to a sitting position.

Outside, the gunfire suddenly stopped. Then Tana heard the sound of more cars arriving in the parking lot.

Through the shattered glass she saw two dozen more cartel gunmen leap from their vehicles. She felt a hand on her arm and turned to see Belasko at her side. Without speaking, he jerked her to her feet and pointed toward the door to the stairs.

As they reached the first step, glass broke behind them. Two men carrying machine guns dived through the windows, hit the floor and rolled.

Bolan squeezed the trigger of his gun twice, and the men stopped rolling.

The big man pushed her and Reuben up the stairs ahead of him, pausing to fire behind him as he went. At the top of the stairs stood a closed door. He moved past the Gonzalezes, kicked, and the door swung inward.

They raced through as another cartel gunner reached the bottom of the stairs. He fired his weapon, the bullet whizzing past Tana's head and through the room. Bolan's Desert Eagle jumped twice in his hand, and a soft moan came from out of sight at the bottom of the stairs.

Tana glanced around the empty bedroom. It was furnished in period pieces, a brass four-poster canopy bed against the wall, an antique bureau in the corner. A simple wooden table next to the bed held a clay water jug, cups and a cast-iron chamber pot.

More stairs led to the third floor.

Bolan fired three more times down the steps, then slammed the door. Pushing Reuben and Tana from behind, he vaulted past them again and kicked the door at the top of the landing.

A faint gasp came from the bed as a young man and woman jackknifed for the blanket at the foot of the mattress. Tana watched the woman's face turn beet red as she scrambled to cover her naked breasts.

The Executioner turned to the couple as he ripped open the door to the roof. "Get in the closet!" he ordered.

The young couple forgot their modesty as they leapt from the bed and disappeared into the tiny room.

Footsteps pounded on the creaking stairs below as the trio raced to the top of Pedro Castle. Bolan swung open the trapdoor and pushed Tana through to the tar-covered roof. Reuben followed, falling to the tar in exhaustion.

Bolan climbed out last and slammed the trapdoor behind him.

There was nowhere left to run.

A three-foot wall circled the roof. Bolan rose to his knees, peering over the edge to the parking lot below. Two dozen cartel hitters squatted behind cars parked haphazardly on the blacktop. They stared toward the canopy-covered entrance and the windows next to it.

Good. They thought he and the Gonzalezes were still downstairs.

The Executioner crawled back to the center of the roof. He looked at Reuben. The man sat panting to one side of the trapdoor, his SIG-Sauer gripped in both hands.

Bolan grabbed the man by the shoulder and shook him gently. "How do you feel?"

Reuben looked up, his eyes glassy. "Dizzy, but I'll be all right."

The stairs creaked as cautious feet mounted the steps beneath the trapdoor.

"Reuben," Bolan said quickly, "you've got to hold them off from here. I'm going to find a way down. Our only chance is to catch them in a cross fire."

The DEA man stared at him, then nodded.

The warrior squatted next to the trapdoor and fired two rounds through the rotting wood. A soft moan floated upward, followed by dull thuds as the body bounced down the steps. Inching the trapdoor open, the Executioner yanked one of the smoke grenades from his harness and pulled the pin. He dropped it through the crevice, then slid the cover back in place. "That ought to slow them down some," he told Reuben.

Gonzalez stared back at him blankly. Maybe he'd heard, maybe he hadn't.

Bolan reholstered the Desert Eagle, dropped to his hands and walked on all fours back to the edge of the roof. He looked over the edge to see that the men in the parking lot still stared toward the dining room.

Drawing the Beretta from shoulder leather, the Executioner raised it slightly over the side of the stone ridge.

Most of the cartel gunners below were grouped behind three cars at the center of the lot. A few others had taken up positions behind other vehicles. All were safe from fire from the dining room.

But not from Bolan's new vantage point.

He leveled the 93-R on the forehead of a gunman at the rear of the lot and squeezed the trigger. When a third eye appeared on the right side of the man's head he fell to the ground.

None of the other cartel hitters noticed.

The Executioner swung the Beretta to a thin man who'd discarded his dress shirt. He squatted behind the engine block of a Datsun, two cars away from the main body of gunners. The man's sweat-soaked, ribbed undershirt stuck to his skinny chest.

Bolan aimed at the guy's heart. A moment later a bright red hole appeared in the undershirt, and blood bubbled from the puncture as the man slid noiselessly to the ground.

The warrior moved the Beretta's front sights to the main body of men. At the far left end, a thick man wore a straw panama hat pulled low over his eyes. He knelt on one knee behind a Toyota Celica, the barrel of an AK-47 pointing toward the sky.

Bolan tapped the trigger, and the hat flew to the ground. The top half of the man's head went with it.

This time the shot drew the attention of the other gunners.

The warrior ripped one of the fragmentation grenades from his battle harness. He held it low, jerking the pin with the other hand, then lobbed it over the edge of the building. As it fell to the earth, he heard the excited voices below.

He counted three, then rose from behind the ledge. As the fragger detonated, he fired down into the midst of the carnage, hitting a fleeing gunner in the stomach and chest with two 9 mm hollowpoints.

The Toyota burst into flame. A moment later a second explosion rocked the night as the gas tank ignited. Bolan fired straight down as seven of the cartel hitters raced from the cars to the shelter of the castle. He dropped three as they ran, two more disappearing under the canopy. The last two dived through the broken glass of the windows.

More men raced for the trees. One hitter, his body ablaze, plodded slowly in the direction of the ocean, then collapsed in a curling black fireball on the lawn.

The Executioner rammed a fresh mag up the 93-R and shoved it back under his arm. He took a deep breath, then looked down at the canvas canopy above the door, three floors below.

Climbing to the top of the ledge, he yanked another grenade from his harness, pulled the pin and hurled the bomb to the center of the cars.

As the frag grenade exploded, Bolan dived from the building. He tucked his knees to his chest, flipping onto his back as he fell through the night. He felt his back hit the canvas canopy above the door, breaking his fall. The aluminum support rods bent, then snapped, and he tumbled to the walkway, the canopy folding to the middle over his head.

Bolan dug his way from the canvas, the Desert Eagle extended before him. A lone gunman remained in the parking lot, firing a MAC-10 from behind a Chevy.

The warrior snap-fired as he raced into the castle. The big .44 slug shaved across the man's cheek, shattering his jaw. Another round finished the job, boring through the gunner's brain.

Several of the men from the lot were crowded at the foot of the stairs as Bolan tore the screen door from its hinges. At the tail of the group, a hitter with an Uzi twisted and fired.

The Executioner dropped to one knee, letting the 9 mm burst sail over his shoulder. The Eagle screamed twice, jerking in his hand, and the subgunner slammed back into the body of men in the stairwell.

Lowering his head, Bolan sprinted toward the tangled mob and drove a shoulder into the man with the Uzi, driving him and the men behind him on into the stairwell. He pulled the last frag grenade from his harness and yanked the pin. Lobbing the deadly egg up the steps, he slammed the door and dived to the floor.

Seconds after the explosion, Bolan jumped to his feet. The big door fell to the floor as he opened it, the hinges blown off by the blast.

He raced up the steps, past mangled bodies and dripping walls, to the second-floor bedroom. He glanced around the corner to the next set of stairs. Empty.

The Executioner pulled back, catching his breath and replacing the Desert Eagle's partially spent magazine with a fresh load from the pouches on his belt. *Empty.* That meant whatever cartel men remained in the castle had to be between the third floor and the roof.

Or on the roof with Reuben and Tana.

Bolan pivoted around the corner and took the steps to the third floor three at a time. As he passed through the bedroom, he saw the closet door open slightly and a nose stuck out.

Then the door slammed shut again.

At least the two young lovers had done as he'd ordered. *They* were safe.

Above him Bolan heard gunfire. He dropped to his knees and peeked around to the stairs. The trapdoor stood open, the stars shining down through the gaping hole. A lone gunman stood near the top, his Browning BDA .380 gripped tightly in both hands, his face a mask of indecision.

Bolan made his decision for him.

Stepping around the corner, the Executioner dropped him with one round under the arm and another massive Magnum slug that entered through the chin and exited through the top of his head.

Slowly, quietly, the warrior crept up the rotting wooden steps. As he reached the top, he pressed his back against the cold stone wall. Three steps from the top, he looked up and whispered through the open trap. "Reuben?"

"Come on up," Tana replied.

Bolan stuck his head through the hole. Reuben Gonzalez sat near the center of the roof, his legs extended in front of him, his eyes staring straight ahead.

The DEA-issue SIG-Sauer was aimed at the Executioner's chest.

Three cartel men lay at Reuben's feet, their bodies dripping crimson from numerous wounds.

Tana sat next to her husband on the tar, her arm crooked through his.

Bolan pulled them to their feet, leading them quickly down the stairs, through the guest room to the dining room. The men and women huddled in the corner had begun rising to their feet, whispering to one another, trying to figure out just what had gone on around them.

They dropped back to the floor as Bolan and the Gonzalezes descended the stairs.

Through the windows the Executioner could see several of the cars in the parking lot still burning. He led the way through the screen, over the fallen awning, to the asphalt. A few halfhearted shots came their way from the bushes and trees but for the most part the remaining cartel hitters wanted no more contact.

Sprinting past the flaming vehicles, Bolan spotted a Cadillac Seville that had skidded to a halt sideways across the yellow parking lines. The keys dangled from the ignition.

The Executioner ushered Reuben into the car. The DEA man collapsed across the back seat; Tana slid across the seat to the passenger side. Bolan cranked the engine and pulled onto the blacktop leading to the highway.

"Where are we going?" Tana asked.

Bolan frowned into the rearview mirror as the headlights of two vehicles from the parking lot appeared. "The airport," he said. "We'll have to make it on our own."

He glanced quickly to the passing line of cedars where he'd hidden the Valmet, MAC and the rest of the weapons. He'd like to have them on the ride to Owen Roberts.

The Executioner stared back at the pursuing cars. You didn't get everything you wanted in life.

The two cars behind him kept a steady pace, not closing the gap, but not falling behind, either.

The Executioner reached the gas station and turned left, the tires screeching as he pointed the Caddie toward George Town and the airport.

The strong, pungent odor of seaweed and saltwater assaulted the Executioner's nostrils as they raced past a sign announcing Milford's Bay. Headlights rounded a curve ahead, and he saw a Ford LTD bearing down in the oncoming lane.

The warrior reached under his fatigue jacket, his fingers closing around the grip of the Beretta 93-R.

The LTD sped past. In the quick flash of headlights, the Executioner recognized the face under the Alaskan bush pilot's cap.

Grimaldi. He hadn't seen them.

The road cut inland again, away from the sea. Ahead, on the straightaway leading to Red Bay, Bolan saw a half-dozen cars approaching in the oncoming lane. He glanced over his shoulder to the back seat.

Reuben Gonzalez's head had fallen forward to his chest. He snored softly.

Bolan reached behind him, tapping the DEA man on the shoulder. "Get him awake," he ordered Tana.

The woman grasped her husband's arms and shook him roughly.

The cars behind increased speed, closing the distance.

Bolan hit the brakes as the lead vehicle in the oncoming convoy screeched to halt, broadside, in front of them. The Caddie skidded down the highway, fishtailing onto the narrow shoulder past the car, then stalled in front of a Datsun that stood second in line.

The warrior leapt from the vehicle as rifle barrels poked through the car windows. He lay a quick 3-round burst across the hood of the Datsun, taking out the windshield, driver and man in the passenger seat. The shadows of two men in the back seat dropped under the fire.

From the corner of his eye, the Executioner saw Reuben and Tana roll from the Caddie. "Hit the bush!" he yelled as he turned back toward the lead vehicle.

Three men exited the car as he turned. They wore camouflage fatigues, and each gripped an M-16.

The driver rested his weapon across the roof of the car, aiming toward Reuben and Tana as they raced toward the jungle.

Bolan swung the Beretta his way, hip-shooting, the round striking the man just under the arm.

The Executioner dropped the other two in turn with a single shot from the 93-R, then turned back toward the other cars in the convoy as they ground to a halt. He ran the Beretta dry, firing into the oncoming vehicles, then shoved it back in the shoulder rig, his hand finding the big Desert Eagle.

Three cars down the line, the Executioner saw a cream-colored limo jerk to a stop. A man in a light silk suit jumped from the back seat. Moonlight fell on his face, reflecting off a long white scar. "Cha-cha!" the man screamed, laying down three rounds toward Reuben and his wife.

Bolan fired two .44s, driving the man back to the rear of the limo.

Reuben and Tana hit the edge of the jungle as leaves and vines jerked from a massive barrage of gunfire. The Executioner fired four rounds from the Desert Eagle into two men in the third car, then took off across the road toward the trees.

He bent low, his left hand scooping up a fallen M-16 on the run, more fire whizzing past his head as he neared the foliage. Twisting to fire a final round from the Desert Eagle, the warrior disappeared into the trees.

He pushed the Gonzalezes farther into the dense jungle. "Keep moving!" he ordered. "I'll catch up." He turned back toward the road as two cartel gunners cautiously appeared at the edge of the tree line.

The Executioner pulled back on the M-16's trigger, detonating a 3-round burst. The first two rounds hit a man wearing cammies squarely in the chest. The final round entered the left eye socket of his partner, then exited. Both men dropped to the ground, dead.

Through the trees Bolan saw three more men slow as they neared the jungle, not anxious to experience the same fate as their comrades. He fired another burst from the M-16, driving them back behind the cars.

From the road the Executioner heard the voice of the scar-faced man in the silk suit. "Cha-cha! I'll kill you *myself!*"

The Executioner fired a final burst toward the road, turned and took off after Reuben and Tana.

6

Jack Grimaldi hit the turn signal and guided the Ford LTD off the highway onto the blacktop. The faint scent of smoke drifted into his nostrils.

He leaned forward, pressing the gas pedal closer to the floor. As he neared the castle, the odor grew. Then he spotted flames leaping through the darkness in the distance.

Grimaldi pulled into the parking lot and hit the brakes. The fiery skeletons of three cars sat on the asphalt, burning like the remnants of ancient ships attacked by privateers.

He threw the Ford into Park. Bodies littered the lot and the patio. A curling mass that had once been human lay on the ground near the sea. The remains of another man, his hand still gripping a weapon, lay on top of the fallen canopy in front of the castle's main entrance. Half-in, half-out of the door that led to a dining room, the body leaked blood from head and chest.

Grimaldi watched as four haggard men sprinted from the trees near the sea. They jumped into a Plymouth and a Volkswagen van, then tore tread from the tires as they rushed away from the carnage.

The pilot left the engine running, opened the door and stepped out of the vehicle. Quickly he passed between the remains of cars, noting the signs of frag grenade shrapnel on the ones not burning.

Stepping over the body in the doorway, Grimaldi entered the castle to find several near-hysterical people dusting themselves off. He approached a man wearing a white dinner jacket and black tie. "What happened?" he asked bluntly.

The man looked at him, a faraway, shocked expression covering his features. "Damned if I know," he said. "One minute we're ordering turtle steak, the next minute everybody starts shooting."

Grimaldi walked back outside. At a table on the patio, in the middle of a mass of shattered beer bottles, sat an old man with a baseball cap and ragged gray beard.

The pilot approached him. "You see what happened?"

The old man nodded.

Grimaldi waited. Finally he said, "Well?"

The gray-bearded man stared toward the pilot's front pants pocket, then he raised his hand, rubbing his thumb back and forth across his first two fingers. "Times is hard."

Grimaldi pulled a Cayman Island twenty-five-dollar bill from his khakis and pressed it into the wrinkled hand. "This should make times a little easier."

"Some cars pulled up in the lot," the old man said. "A man comes to my table. He's lookin' for his mates, two men and a woman. He describes the woman. She little. Yellow hair. He asks have I seen her. I just see her goin' in the bar, so's I tell him as much. The next thing I know, guns are explodin', and I'm under the table."

Grimaldi slipped the old man another bill. "Anyone get hit?"

The old man looked up at him like he'd just seen the dead rise and walk. "Look around ye, mate."

Grimaldi shook his head. "No. Of the two men and the woman."

The old man shrugged. "Think not," he said. "They drove off in one of the cars."

Grimaldi turned back to the Ford. Brass casings and broken glass crunched under his feet as he walked past the simmering cars and burned and broken bodies on the ground.

As he approached the LTD, he heard the faint, sharp cracks of gunfire somewhere in the distance. The sounds faded, then resumed, and the pilot stared off through the trees to the highway, back in the direction from which he'd come.

Striker was alive, all right. Somewhere back on the road.

Grimaldi kicked himself mentally as he broke into a run toward the car. He had to have passed them on the highway as he drove to the castle.

Sliding behind the wheel, Stony Man's ace pilot threw the Ford into Drive and floored the accelerator, cutting from the parking lot back to the blacktop road.

He was halfway to the highway when three police cars, sirens wailing and lights piercing the darkness, rounded the corner and came toward him.

The lead car pulled over into his lane and stopped.

Grimaldi brought the car to a halt, his mind racing, working out his story. His spirits took a nosedive as he saw the tall, burly black man exit the first squad car, toting a Remington 870 pump-action shotgun.

Captain Bodden's brawny forearms shook slightly as his fingers fumbled to find the safety on the unfamiliar weapon.

Grimaldi waited.

The policeman walked cautiously up to the window. He rested the barrel of the pump gun on the door, aimed at Grimaldi's throat. His big head nodded up and down under the pith helmet, his face a blank deadpan. "You again."

Bodden stepped away from the Ford, holding the shotgun tightly in both hands. "Step out of the car."

Slowly Grimaldi did as he was told.

Suddenly the weight of the Smith & Wesson .357 in the clip holster at the small of the pilot's back reminded him he was about to have trouble—more trouble than he'd counted on.

He glanced back at the open door of the Ford. It was too late to ditch the gun under the seat.

"Why do you always appear at the scene of a shooting?" Bodden asked. "Shootings that didn't occur before your arrival on the island?"

Grimaldi shrugged. "Bad luck, I guess. Believe me, this isn't any more fun for me than you."

"Why are you here?" the big captain repeated.

"Captain Bodden," Grimaldi said, "I just came out here for dinner. Heard they had good—" the pilot racked his brain for what the man in the dinner jacket had said he'd ordered "—turtle steak."

Bodden stared at him. "I don't think I believe you," he said. "Turn around. Place your hands on top of the automobile."

Grimaldi turned around. It would be a matter of seconds now. The big black man would find the Smith, and he'd be handcuffed and on his way to jail.

Striker and the Gonzalezes would have no way off the island. Worse, they'd have no way of knowing he'd been arrested so they could try another route.

He felt the barrel of the Remington press into the back of his neck. Then the big black man's hands ran up his calves, the front and backs of his thighs, then around to his belt buckle. As the hands moved rearward, toward the pistol at the small of his back, the pilot made his decision.

He and Striker had been through the wars together. The man known as the Executioner had saved his life more times than he could remember. He couldn't let the big guy down now that Bolan needed him.

Grimaldi felt Bodden's hands stop as they felt the pistol in his belt, heard the man take a sudden, deep breath. The barrel of the Remington pressed harder into his neck.

Grimaldi spun as the big hand fumbled for the gun under his shirt. Driving his arm up and around, he caught the barrel of the shotgun with an elbow, moving it two inches to the side of his head as it discharged.

The pilot's head rang as if it was inside a church bell as he continued his spin, driving his fist into Bodden's jaw.

The big man staggered back, the shotgun falling from his hands.

Then Grimaldi was off, sprinting for the cedar trees on the other side of the blacktop. He heard Bodden curse. Then the shotgun exploded again, and the leaves shook three feet to his side as he entered the cedars.

More fire sounded to his rear as Grimaldi cut through the trees. He wondered where he was heading, and if he'd make it.

BOLAN PAUSED periodically, listening for sounds of pursuit as they hurried away from the highway. Each time the trees shook behind them, the Executioner turned, scattering a few rounds to the rear.

Soon the noises faded altogether.

The warrior led them deeper into the jungle. The cartel's withdrawal made sense, he realized as he chopped a path through the darkened jungle. New blood had arrived on the island during the day. That was evident in the camouflaged men with the M-16s they'd just encountered.

By now the Lima cartel had enough men on Grand Cayman to encircle the interior and patrol the highway that ran the circumference of the island. They no longer needed to track their prey through the jungle.

Bolan and the Gonzalezes would have to emerge eventually.

The Executioner stopped as they neared the edge of a large marshland, continuing to evaluate the cartel's position. The Peruvians had outgunned the Cayman Island police since their arrival early that morning. And now the men from Lima had enough troops to outnumber them, as well. Sooner or later the cartel hitters would meet up with those undergunned officers, and the results of that meeting would be disastrous.

Unless the island officials changed their minds about American intervention, the deaths of dozens of police officers would be on their heads.

Bolan turned to Reuben as they reached the marshland. The little man's bandanna had slipped to the side, revealing the white bloodstained bandage around his head. "How you feeling?"

"Tired," Reuben replied. "But the pain's gone. At least for now."

Bolan nodded and turned to Tana. "How about you?"

"Depressed."

Bolan couldn't suppress a laugh. He couldn't help liking the woman. She was doing her best in a world she didn't understand. "Depression's understandable, under the circumstances."

"And I'm *hungry*."

He smiled at her through the moonlight. "We'll cross the open area, then pitch camp for the night. We'll eat then."

Tana stared up at him in awe. "Eat?" She pointed to his buttpack. "I suppose you've got a microwave in there."

"Wait and see."

The full moon shone down over the marshland as Bolan led the way across the swamp, crawling on hands and knees through the grassy mud. He glanced over his shoulder twice, checking on Reuben and Tana. He watched the woman try to wipe the mud and grass from her face as she moved along.

She was holding up well. So was Reuben.

They still had a chance.

Entering the thick vegetation again, the Executioner led them twenty yards to a small break in the trees. "We'll camp here for the night," he whispered. He slid the buttpack around to his front and unzipped it. Pulling three small rectangles from the pack, he handed them to Reuben.

"What're those?" the DEA man asked.

"Space blankets," Bolan answered. "Unfold them—cammie-side out—and spread them out." He turned to Tana. "You might want to gather some leaves to put under them."

Tana began scooping up green leaves, dropping them into piles and smoothing them along the ground while Reuben unfolded the blankets.

Bolan retraced his steps toward the swamp, remembering an almond tree they'd passed a few minutes before. Quickly he stuffed his pockets with the nuts.

Returning to camp, he saw that Reuben had begun breaking dried limbs into kindling. Bolan shook his head. "No fire."

A few yards on the other side of the campsite, the warrior found a breadfruit tree. As he pulled the sweet fruit from the limbs, his eyes fell on an avocado tree growing wild in the jungle.

His fatigue jacket heavy with fruit and nuts, Bolan returned to camp. Reuben and Tana sat on the make-shift beds, looking up expectantly.

He dropped cross-legged to the ground and began piling the almonds, avocados and breadfruit on the space blanket in front of him. Reaching into his butt-pack once more, he produced two long lengths of beef jerky and a half-dozen Tiger's Milk Nutrition Bars. "Soup's on."

Reuben stared in amazement at the pile of food before them. He looked up at the Executioner, his dirty, unshaven face breaking into a grin in the moonlight. "You forgot the freeze-dried wine."

Bolan chuckled. He unhooked the canteen from his belt, twisted the cap and handed it to the man. "Just have to make do, I guess."

Using the pliers of his Leatherman Pocket Tool, Bolan began cracking almonds. Reuben and Tana downed breadfruit and jerky as if they hadn't eaten for weeks.

Reuben finished an avocado and dropped the seed to the ground. He leaned back, supporting himself with his elbows, and stared at the sky. He was doing far better now, and the Executioner wondered if he might have overestimated the extent of the man's injuries. It was still too early to tell.

"How's the head?" Bolan asked.

"Hurts a little," the DEA agent answered, "but it's my heart that gives me the real pain."

Bolan didn't reply. The man was leading to something, wanted to get something off his chest. If he needed to badly enough, he'd do so without any prompting from the Executioner.

"The man back at the highway," Reuben finally said. "The one in the white suit, with the scar, who called out my name. You remember him?"

Bolan cracked another almond and thought back to the man with the nickel-plated Colt. There was no doubt in his mind that he'd been in charge of the cartel gunners. "Yes."

"His name is Marino Mariategui," Reuben said. "A midlevel boss for the Peruvians. I was duked into him by his brother-in-law, our snitch." Reuben shifted on the blanket, gingerly fingered the bandage on his forehead, then continued. "I'd met him briefly, a while back in Colombia. I was undercover, working as a courier for a guy named Juan Montoya. Marino was an enforcer."

Bolan looked up. He remembered Montoya well. A top Colombian general, Montoya had hooked up with Fidel Castro with plans to ship massive quantities of cocaine into the U.S.

Then they'd met the Executioner.

"He didn't recognize you?" Bolan asked.

"Vaguely," Reuben said. "But it didn't matter. He only remembered seeing me in Montoya's company. I was never burned in Colombia. The investigation was scrapped because Montoya fled the country after parties unknown raised hell in his organization.

"With the vague memory of me in Medellín," Reuben continued, "and his brother-in-law's introduction, Mariategui welcomed me with open arms."

"So how'd you get burned?" Bolan asked.

Reuben shrugged. "Stupid, really. I'd only seen Tana three times in two years. We met for weekends in Brazil. I missed her like hell." Reuben paused. His eyes dropped to the ground, and he blew air through his closed lips, making them flutter up and down. "She wanted to move down, and I wanted her to. My judgment got a little clouded." He took a deep breath. "I had to tell Marino *something,* so I said that a woman I knew from America was coming to live with me. The cartel had checked my background, or rather that of 'Cha-cha Pasquela.' No problem. DEA had covered me well."

Bolan put it together himself. "But not her."

"No. She wasn't supposed to come to Lima. I'd have had to get special clearance from the *segundo*— that's the deputy director—and he'd have never allowed it."

Tana looked up, her face showing her guilt. "I just missed him so much," she said quietly. "We didn't think . . ."

Reuben leaned over and squeezed her knee. "Exactly. We didn't think."

"So that's what's bothering you?" Bolan asked.

"That's part of it. I'll catch hell for that as soon as I get back, but there's more."

Bolan studied the weary face silently.

"It may sound strange, but Marino and I were friends."

"You did your job, Reuben," Bolan said, "and Mariategui wasn't your friend."

"Yes, I suppose," he agreed hesitantly. "Yeah, it's my job. But this time it was different. I know it doesn't make sense, Belasko, but Marino and I became like brothers. I couldn't help but like the guy. We hunted together. Fished. I ate dinner at least once a week with him and his wife. It was like I was a member of the family." He turned to face Bolan in the darkness. "Marino Mariategui and I did more than route drugs together. The man was more than just a dope pusher."

The Executioner didn't speak. He thought of the countless undercover cops he'd worked with over the years. What Reuben was experiencing was a common malady among them. Working undercover too long changed an agent's perspective. He tended to lose his identity as a cop and drift in a semilighted limbo, somewhere between the real world and the one he'd created.

Finally Bolan broke the silence. "The bottom line, Reuben, is the man sells drugs, drugs that kill men, women and children. The man sells death." He paused and drew in a breath. "Now, from where I sit, the fact that he was fun to go fishing with doesn't excuse that. What do you think?"

"No, of course not," the DEA man said quickly. "It's just . . . Marino had another side. He was intelligent. Even kind and gentle at times."

"Sure," Bolan said. "Hitler built good highways, Mussolini made the trains run on time and Marino Mariategui could be kind and gentle. How much kindness does it take to sell poison to people? And when he was an enforcer for Montoya and murdered people, did he do it gently?''

Reuben flinched slightly. "Yes, of course. You're right. It's just that I knew him, Belasko. You didn't. He came from a good family. He was educated. Marino had the ability to be so much more. He could have been something different. Something good."

"But he didn't choose that road, Reuben, which makes him all the more guilty in my book. The man doesn't even have an excuse. He wasn't forced into drug dealing by economics or anything else. He did it out of greed, pure and simple."

Reuben leaned forward, his shoulders drooping slightly. "I agree with you in my head, Belasko. It's my heart that continues to argue."

Reuben pulled a blade of grass from the ground and stuck it in his mouth. "I don't know," he said. "Maybe what bothers me even more is that I busted the assignment. Mariategui's as high up the ladder as I got. And believe me, Belasko, Marino's only a medium-sized fish in a big pond. Slamming the barred door on him and a few of the others may put a damper on the Lima cartel's operations. For a while. But before you know it, it'll be business as usual in Peru." The DEA man looked up at the stars overhead. "And if I hadn't blown it, I might have gotten the big fish."

"And who's that?" Bolan asked.

The agent shrugged. "A guy by the name of Hector Pizarro. Not that it matters much now."

Bolan filed the information in the back of his mind for future reference.

Reuben looked at Tana, who sat fumbling with the wrapper of a Tiger's Milk bar. Slowly the DEA man reached over and took it from her. He tore open the foil, then handed it back. "I blew it, Belasko, and I endangered the life of the only woman I've ever loved," he said.

Tana looked up.

"I should never have allowed you to come to Peru," Reuben said.

"You didn't have any choice," she replied. "I'd have come even if you told me not to. I missed you, too, you know. We've been separated too much over the years, and I'm sick of it. I came to be with *you,* and I'd do it again—whether you like it or not."

As the parrots chattered in the treetops and the wind whistled through the leaves, Reuben and Tana Gonzalez lay back on their space blankets, arm in arm. Soon Bolan heard the steady sound of Reuben snoring.

Minutes later the warrior heard movement in the trees to his left. Drawing the All Terrain Chopper from its sheath, he rose silently and moved toward the sound. As he peered through the darkness, he saw an agouti rabbit feeding on a fallen breadfruit. The small animal looked up at the Executioner as he approached, then lowered its head and continued eating.

Bolan returned to camp and took a seat with his back against the trunk of a buttonwood tree. He stared across the clearing to Reuben and Tana. They slept peacefully in each other's arms. The Executioner closed his eyes, but he didn't sleep.

BOLAN PULLED the partially spent 9 mm and .44 magazines from their pouches, consolidating the remaining rounds and discarding the empty clips. As the night drew on, he considered their options.

He could bypass the call to Grimaldi, leading Reuben and Tana directly to the airport and establishing contact with the Stony Man pilot once they were there. But that would involve either one or all of them entering the terminal. He glanced down at his own muck-covered fatigues, then to the mud-stiff clothes of the sleeping couple.

They looked great for hiding out in the woods. The mud just added to the camouflage effect and helped them blend into the terrain. But walking through the airport dressed as they were would raise a few eyebrows—eyebrows that might well belong to the Peruvians.

Besides, Mariategui would have the heaviest concentration of men at the airport, knowing it was their only means of escape. He'd know they weren't likely to make a break for it across the sea. Grand Cayman floated in the middle of the Caribbean. The nearest land were the two sister islands of Cayman Brac and Little Cayman, eighty miles away. To leave either by air meant rerouting back to Owen Roberts airport.

And the next nearest land was Cuba.

No, Bolan realized as he listened to a heron cry in the distance, they'd be better off coming out of the jungle somewhere they weren't expected, someplace that would be lightly patrolled by the Peruvians.

And someplace where they could gain access to a phone. Unseen, this time.

The Executioner unfolded his map, studying it in the light of a small flashlight. At the northeast corner of the east side of the island, just before North Sound but south, he saw Rum Point. A little farther west lay a development area known as Cayman Kai—vacation houses, with phones. And at least some of the houses were bound to be empty.

He stuffed the map back in his pack and finished reloading the gun magazines.

Two hours before sunrise the Executioner woke Reuben and Tana. They both moved slowly, stiffly, sluggish in their movements as they struggled to their feet. The wear and tear of the day before was taking its toll. Their exhaustion couldn't be erased by a few hours' sleep.

Bolan gave them both a Tiger's Milk quick-energy bar. He waited while they ate, then handed Tana the canteen.

As she tipped it to her lips, Reuben winked at the Executioner, then turned to his wife. "You forgot to make the coffee again?" he asked.

Tana made a face and handed him the water container. "Do I have to do everything around here?" she chided. She pointed down at a pile of almond shells on the ground. "It's your job to take out the trash."

Bolan scattered the shells and other debris around the camp. He wanted no evidence left that might be found by any cartel patrols still circulating through the interior. He watched Reuben take a last drink of water, then look to his wife again.

"What the hell, honey," the agent said. "I always promised you an exotic island vacation, didn't I?"

Tana smiled. "I'd have preferred a cruise. This is a little more exotic than I'd planned."

Bolan rehooked the canteen to his belt. Their spirits were higher after the rest, and they were still keeping each other going. That was good. The Executioner refolded the space blankets into his buttpack. But high spirits and positive attitudes had their limits, and he wondered how long it would last.

He gathered the Tiger's Milk wrappers and threw them with the avocado seeds into a small depression in the damp soil. He brushed leaves over the top with his boot.

The Executioner ushered them again through the jungle, chopping a path northeast through the thick vegetation. An hour later a vast open swampland appeared through the trees to the north. Back to the west the waters of North Sound sparkled under the early-morning moon.

"We've got to cross the marsh before the sun comes up," Bolan whispered in the darkness. "It's almost three miles. You two up to it?"

They nodded.

He led them out onto the soggy earth as the moon dropped lower on the horizon. They walked quietly through the muddy bog, the only sounds the sucking noise each time their feet rose from the semisolid slough.

The sun peeked up in the east as they neared a small forest area on the far north side of the island. To his left Bolan saw the waters of North Sound more clearly now. Somewhere across the sound lay Owen Roberts airport, Jack Grimaldi and safety.

They followed the tree line west, along the road, toward several beach houses in the distance. As they neared the first house, a large sign sprang up across the road: Cayman Kai Beach Houses—Island Homes Away From Home.

Bolan stopped them across from the first house. He looked up and down the highway, then started out of the trees. The sound of a car approaching from the east drove him back to cover.

Bolan and the Gonzalezes squatted in the brush as a long sedan bearing four unshaven men in camouflage shirts drove slowly by, scanning the roadside.

The Executioner watched as they passed out of sight around a curve, then turned to Reuben and Tana. "Let's go," he whispered.

They hurried across the road into the front yard. They passed a smaller sign mounted on a post driven into the ground. Melka's Mini-Mansion, it read. Leon and Lois Melka, Chicago, Illinois.

Bolan and the Gonzalezes sprinted by the sign to a door at the side of the house. The warrior scanned the beach. Satisfied that they hadn't been spotted, he moved to the door. Jamming his hand down into the billow pocket of his fatigue jacket, he drove his cloth-covered fist through the rectangle of glass nearest the doorknob. The glass tinkled quietly as it fell to the concrete.

The warrior reached through the window, unlocked the door and guided Reuben and Tana into the house. With a final glance outside, he ducked in after them.

They entered a laundry room, moving quickly past a washing machine on one side and a dryer on the other, and crossed into the kitchen. The stale odor of death hit the Executioner's nose like a baseball bat. He looked down to see a half dozen dead and rotting mice in "glue-traps" on the floor by the refrigerator.

The hind legs of the animals had been jerked from their sockets as they raced across the sticky surface toward the bait. Their moldering carcasses lay grotesquely misshapen on the viscous pads.

The Executioner ran his hand along the kitchen counter as he walked briskly toward the living room. A thick film of dust came away on his palm.

More dust covered the furniture in the living room. He glanced to the bookshelf. A framed picture showed the Melkas standing outside the front door of the house.

Lois Melka, short and gray haired, looked to be in her early sixties. She was casually yet immaculately dressed, her makeup perfect. An impish smile covered her face as she smiled into the camera.

The picture told Bolan what he needed to know. The Melkas weren't around. Mrs. Melka wasn't the type of woman who left dead mice rotting in the traps. Dust didn't build up in *her* kitchen.

The Executioner turned to Reuben and Tana. They both searched frantically through the cabinets in the kitchen. Tana located the glasses and they moved to the sink, drinking as if it had been weeks, rather than days, that they'd been in the bush.

Tana looked toward him, her face suddenly reddening in embarrassment. Grabbing another glass from the cabinet, she filled it from the tap and took it to him.

"Thanks." Bolan took the water, emptied the glass, then yanked the canteen from his belt and handed both receptacles back to the woman. "Fill this first, then make yourselves comfortable. I'll call the airport."

As Tana filled the canteen, the Executioner moved to the phone on an end table next to a stuffed reclining chair. Dialing the airport, he asked for Bob Wolfe once again.

Tana handed him the filled canteen as he waited. The woman moved confidently about the living room, studying the paintings on the walls and then taking a seat across from Bolan on the couch.

Reuben took a seat next to her and draped an arm around her shoulder. "It's almost over, honey," he said.

Bolan heard a click on the other end of the line, then a thick Caymanian accent said, "May I help you?"

The Executioner hesitated. "Mr. Wolfe," he finally said. "I'm paging Bob Wolfe."

"Mr. Wolfe has been called away from the airport. He asked that I speak with you. If you will tell me where you are—"

Bolan hung up, then stood. He opened the wide glass door and walked out onto the porch. Hooked to large brass O-rings mounted in the walls, a striped hammock swung gently in the early-morning breeze. Nailed to a support post in the center of the porch was a dartboard, and the picture of someone the Melkas evidently didn't care for had been thumb-tacked to the center of the cork.

Bolan glanced over the incoming waves to a fishing boat trolling a hundred yards from shore.

Where the hell was Grimaldi?

There were only two possible answers. The first was that the pilot had been captured or killed by cartel gunmen. That didn't seem likely. They had no way of knowing who he was.

The second possibility was that the police had seen him at both the Tortuga Club and then Pedro Castle. Grand Cayman was a peaceful island. A strange American face arriving at both sites immediately after gunfights would seem like too much of a coincidence to the police.

Bolan felt himself nodding silently as one of the fishermen cast another line over the side of the boat. Jack Grimaldi was either dead, had been taken into custody for questioning, or was on the run.

If the Stony Man pilot had died in the course of the mission, there was nothing the Executioner could do now. There would be time for grief—and paybacks—later.

And if his problems were police related, that was Brognola's department. The Justice man could take care of the diplomatic end of things when the shooting stopped.

Bolan glanced back at the Gonzalezes, sitting happily hand in hand on the couch behind him. Relief beamed across both of their faces.

They thought their time in hell was over.

The Executioner turned back to the sea. He was afraid it had just begun.

7

Something was wrong. He hadn't talked to Bob Wolfe. Tana watched as the big man stood and walked to the couch, looked down at them. "Change in plans," he said.

Tana felt her heart jump.

"I'll give it to you straight," he went on. "I don't know what's happened exactly, but my pilot didn't answer the page at the airport."

"Maybe he was just out for something," Reuben suggested.

"He might have been in the rest room," Tana heard herself say hopefully.

Bolan shook his head, dismissing the possibilities. "Not this guy. I know him. If something wasn't wrong, he'd have been within arm's reach of the phone. I'm not sure what's happened, but what it amounts to is we're on our own again."

"So what do we do now?" Reuben asked.

"For now, we rest some more. Nobody slept very well last night, me included."

Tana waited for Belasko to continue. She and Reuben might not have slept *well* last night, but he hadn't slept at all. She had awakened several times during the night to see him sitting against a tree, his eyes scanning the darkness.

"We're going to have to make it off the island on our own," the big man finally said. "And that probably means a lot more jungle and a lot more swamp. We'll all need to be rested."

Tana watched him. What he meant was *they* would need to be rested. There was a strength within this man that she'd never seen before in any other human being. It was the same type of strength Reuben had, but in Belasko it was magnified a thousand times. He seemed capable of going on without sleep. Maybe not forever, but certainly past the point when most people would drop in their tracks.

"As long as they don't spot us, we're probably as safe in this house as anywhere on Grand Cayman," he continued. "So for right now I want you two to go upstairs. Get cleaned up, find some clean clothing, then get some sleep."

"How about you?" Reuben asked. "You've got to rest sometime, too. I can stand guard while—"

Bolan declined the offer. "You're the one with the head injury. Besides, I've got work to do." He paused. "I want you both to listen to me. We *can* get away from here and back to the U.S., but I won't lie to you. It won't be easy, and it'll take some planning. And to do that, I need to be alone." He pointed toward the stairs. "So let's get on with it."

Tana glanced again to the bookshelf and saw Belasko follow her eyes. Lois Melka smiled back at both of them with a cat-that-ate-the-canary gleam.

"We should wear their clothes?" Tana asked, turning back to Belasko uncomfortably. "Isn't that stealing?"

He hooked a thumb over his shoulder toward the photograph. "Tana," he said, "that lady looks like a woman who'd understand the circumstances."

Tana felt a giggle escape her lips. Then the giggle turned to laughter, then the laughter suddenly became convulsions of near hysteria. She tried to stop but couldn't.

Fear pierced her heart through the hilarity. Why? It wasn't *that* funny, and Belasko might not have meant it as a joke at all. She didn't want to hurt his feelings.

Tana grabbed her sides, trying to stop laughing. She succeeded for a moment, then bent almost double as seizures of glee racked her body once more. She felt tears streaming down her face.

She felt her husband's arm tighten around her shoulders. He drew her closer. "It's all right," he whispered into her ear. "There, now, it's all right."

Suddenly the laughter turned to sobs. She felt her chest heave in and out, sending fire through her lungs with every desperate breath. The wetness streaming down her cheeks became tears of fear, frustration, anguish.

Then Reuben helped her to her feet, circling both arms around her and drawing her against his chest. He hugged her tight against him, and that familiar touch, the powerful hands and arms that had comforted her through seven years of marriage—for better and for worse—stopped the crying.

Tana felt another hand, foreign, unfamiliar, yet comforting as well, on her shoulder. She stared up through her blurred eyes to see the man called Belasko standing next to her.

His face was hard, lined with the memories of battles like the one they now faced. Yet a kindness, gentleness, shone from his eyes, as well. He smiled down at her.

"Go upstairs now," he said quietly. "It'll be all right."

BOLAN SPREAD THE MAP across the dining room table. Upstairs, he heard the sound of running water as the shower started. Good. Getting clean should help Tana's frame of mind.

The Executioner felt himself frown as his thoughts turned to Reuben. The man had been functioning well since morning. Maybe the concussion he'd suffered had been light and the symptoms were beginning to vanish. Tana's near breakdown had brought out a deeper strength within the man, much like the courage the woman had exhibited earlier when Reuben's injuries had made him dependent on *her*.

Above his head Bolan heard the sound of the shower door opening, then closing again. Reuben and Tana had a good marriage. They seemed to function as one unit—each strong in areas in which the other was weak.

Maybe that was what made successful marriages, Bolan thought. He didn't know. His life had taken a course in which marriage—even commitment to another person—hadn't been possible. And in his never-ending war, that was an area of life he wasn't likely to learn much more about.

Bolan turned back to the map. They were roughly a half mile from Rum Point, on the north coast of the island. George Town, and Owen Roberts airport, lay southeast across North Sound. At least a fifteen-mile trek, back through the jungles and marshes through which they'd already come. Maybe seven miles tops, as the crow flew.

A sudden thought struck the Executioner. Seven miles as the crow flew. The same distance as the fish swam.

So far, they'd made their way by land, and unless he missed his guess, it was on land that Mariategui would concentrate his forces. But did they have boats circling the island, as well?

The Executioner thought back to the fishing boat he'd seen earlier in the morning. It might have been just that—a charter craft taking tourists out to snare a few wahoo, grouper or barracuda. On the other hand, it could well have been a cartel vehicle disguised as such.

There was no way of knowing.

The Executioner frowned. He returned to the map. The chart showed a jetty at Rum Point and several buildings, including the Rum Point Club. Unless he missed his guess, it would be very much like the Tortuga Club—a lodge with a bar and several private cottages. The resort would provide charter fishing, sailing...

And scuba diving.

Bolan felt the muscles in his forearms tighten as the plan began to formulate. The Lima cartel had men, planes and automobiles. They might have boats. He'd bet his life they didn't have submarines.

He contemplated the possibilities. He had no idea if Reuben or Tana had ever even been underwater. Even if they were experienced scuba divers, they were in no condition to navigate seven miles across North Sound.

But if he could create a diversion, then drop beneath the sea, it would be as if they'd vanished into thin air.

While the rest of the cartel killers rushed to Rum Point, they could emerge somewhere down the coast, acquire a boat and speed the rest of the way to the airport across the sound.

Bolan's eyes traveled down the map. A little over a mile to the south of Rum Point, a slender finger of land pointed out across North Sound. Water Point. The map's topography showed the point as a mixture of swamp vegetation and areas of low, open growth. Two miles farther south the marsh island of Booby Cay hugged the coast.

If things went well, they could make it to the cay, then follow the marsh again until they found a boat. If not, Bolan felt certain he could at least get them through the water to Water Point. Then perhaps they could still escape by land, while the cartel searched the area north of them.

Bolan folded the map and stuffed it into his butt-pack. The immediate problem would be getting to

Rum Point. They'd already seen the Peruvians patrolling the road.

The Executioner kicked the problem around in his mind as he walked slowly through the living room. He paused at the bookshelf. Next to the photo he'd seen earlier of Leon and Lois Melka stood another framed picture. A younger man, with the features of both parents, smiled back at the camera. The man looked to be fairly good size. Maybe he'd have some clothes that would fit.

Bolan mounted the stairs to the second floor. From the large bedroom to his left, he heard the steady sound of Reuben's breathing as the weary DEA agent slept.

The warrior turned into a small bedroom across the hall. Outside the house he heard the sound of vehicles. He took a seat on the bed and looked down through the window to see a green Plymouth pass, the unshaven faces of four men searching both sides of the road.

No, the road was out of the question. They'd have to reach Rum Point along the beach. And they'd have to look different, dress in the Melkas' clothes.

But it could be done.

From the master bedroom the Executioner heard the bedsprings creak. A moment later a toilet flushed from somewhere deeper within the room.

He rose from the bed and opened the closet door. Inside he found a faded pair of jeans, a cutoff sweatshirt and a ragged pair of canvas deck shoes. Throwing the articles over his arm, he retraced his steps to the downstairs bedroom.

The Executioner dropped the fresh clothes on the bed and entered the adjacent bathroom. He tossed his mud-soaked fatigue jacket to the tiles in the corner, reached inside the stall and turned on the shower. He'd just unbuckled his belt when he heard footsteps on the stairs.

He paused, then Tana stepped into the bedroom. She stopped, staring at him through the open door.

She and Mrs. Melka must have been the same size. The pleated, stone-washed jeans fit her perfectly. Her T-shirt featured a giant, cartoon mosquito. Below the insect were the words Cayman Island National Bird.

"Oh, uh, I'm sorry," Tana stammered, embarrassed. "I, uh..."

Bolan repressed a chuckle. Unless she figured his chest was indecent, he wasn't displaying anything improper. "Don't worry about it," he said, resnapping his pants. "Why aren't you sleeping?"

"I...couldn't. I'm really not that tired anymore. I thought I'd clean up after us a little." She glanced at Bolan's fatigue jacket on the floor. "I hate to dirty the place up for these people."

Bolan nodded. She looked better, more in control. She was probably still too wound up to sleep, and the next best thing would be to keep her busy, keep her mind occupied. "Good idea," he said. "Just stay out of sight from the windows."

Tana smiled. "I'll be careful." She glanced toward the bathroom floor again.

Bolan followed her eyes, picked up the jacket and handed it to her. Tana started to leave the room.

"Wait a second."

She turned back, a puzzled look on her face.

"You and Reuben ever scuba dive before?"

The creases in Tana's forehead deepened. "Reuben has. I took a class at the YMCA a few years ago, but never got out of the swimming pool. Why do you ask?"

Bolan grinned. It was better than nothing. At least she'd had a regulator in her mouth.

"I'll explain later."

The Executioner closed the bathroom door, undressed and stepped into the shower.

TANA GONZALEZ CARRIED Belasko's muddy jacket up the stairs. She paused at the bedroom door, then tiptoed silently across the room, her eyes on her sleeping husband. Reuben looked so peaceful, relaxed.

She bent and kissed him lightly on the forehead, gathered their dirty clothes from the bathroom floor and retraced her steps down the stairs.

She almost gagged as she neared the rotting mice. The stench was almost unbearable. Passing the traps on the floor, she set the clothes on top of the washing machine in the laundry room, then returned to search through the kitchen.

In a drawer next to the sink, she found a box of plastic garbage bags. She held her face away as she lifted the glue-traps from the floor and dropped the decomposed mice into a bag. Twisting the top tightly, she secured it with a serrated plastic retaining strip and set it in the laundry room.

There. The kitchen still smelled like... What was it Reuben always said?—a dead goat's butt. But at least the tiny carcasses weren't around anymore.

Tana opened the cabinet under the sink and looked down. She smiled. She was beginning to feel as though she knew Lois Melka. The sponge, cleaner and a small plastic bucket were right where she'd have put them herself.

She filled the bucket with hot water, added liquid cleaner and dropped to her hands and knees, going to work on the muddy footprints in the kitchen. As she scrubbed her way toward the laundry room, the acrid stench of the decaying mice grew strong again.

Her stomach churned as she rose to her feet and walked past the sack, trying not to gag. She glanced through the tiny windows in the door leading outside and saw a metal trash can sitting ten feet from the exit.

No, Tana told herself. Belasko had warned her to stay away from the windows. And going outside would be just asking for trouble.

Still, the odor...

Tana grabbed the bag and opened the door. She was halfway to the trash can when a green car came slowly down the highway in front of the house.

The woman felt the chill race up her spine. She dropped the trash bag onto the can, then turned, facing the road.

Four hard, cruel-looking faces stared back at her.

Gathering her wits, Tana walked casually back to the house. She had to stay calm, she told herself. Act as if she belonged here. They wouldn't even notice her.

She closed the door behind her and looked back through the glass. The Plymouth continued down the road and out of sight.

Tana breathed a silent sigh of relief. They hadn't paid any attention to her.

Grabbing the sponge and bucket, she climbed the stairs to the bedroom.

Reuben had awakened. He looked better, the fogginess in his eyes having almost gone completely. He stood next to the closet, buttoning the last button of a short-sleeve madras sport shirt.

Tana felt herself grinning as he tucked the shirttail into a pair of burgundy Bermuda shorts. She looked down at his feet. Black socks and gray, Velcro-strap jogging shoes.

"Mr. Melka's quite a dresser," she said. "All you need is some pukka shells around your neck."

Reuben chuckled. "Hey, you take what you can get around here," he said. "It took me ten minutes to find the shoes. Thought I was going to have to wear his wing tips." He pointed to several pairs of heavy leather brogans on the closet floor.

Tana laughed and felt the fear leaving her body. Everything would be all right. Another few hours, and they'd be safely back in America.

She moved past Reuben into the bathroom, knelt by the shower and began scrubbing the walls.

As she ran the sponge over the stall, she stared through the small bathroom window facing the front of the house. A long row of royal palm trees lined the other side of the road. She watched the branches weave in the breeze as she worked. A coconut fell to the ground with a lazy clomp.

The woman squeezed the sponge out in the bucket and dumped the brown water down the drain. Grand Cayman really *was* a beautiful island. It would be nice to come back sometime—a *long* time from now—and see it without people chasing you around and shooting at you.

Tana turned on the shower and watched the last remnants of dirt chase down the drain. She twisted the knob, lifted the bucket and took a final glance out the window to the palms.

She was still watching, hoping another coconut would fall, when the green car turned into the drive, followed by two other vehicles.

BOLAN ZIPPED HIS JEANS, pulled the sweatshirt over his head and stepped into the deck shoes. The shirt stretched tightly over his chest and shoulders. The pants were okay in the waist, but the cuffs stopped above his ankles.

At least the shoes fit reasonably well.

The Executioner lifted his mud-caked fatigue pants from the floor. Pulling several C.I. twenty-five-dollar bills from his wallet, he set them on the nightstand next to the bed.

It was more than enough to cover the broken window and the clothes they were taking.

Bolan glanced to his battle harness, guns and butt-pack. The pack should be no problem, but he'd draw more than a little attention wearing the harness and weapons along the beach. No, he'd have to devise another means to carry the firepower.

An uneasy, intangible feeling hit his gut as he entered the kitchen. Something was different—something had changed. On the counter he saw an open box of black garbage bags. He tore one from the end of the roll and wrapped it around the Beretta and Desert Eagle.

The odd feeling continued as he dumped the battle harness into a second bag. What the hell was it?

He glanced down at the wet spots drying on the floor. Tana had mopped up their footprints.

And the mice were gone.

The warrior's eyes flew instinctively to the back door. Through the broken pane of glass he saw the trash can. Sitting on the top was a garbage bag, a garbage bag that hadn't been there when they arrived.

Bolan hoisted the weapons bags and sprinted to the stairs. Taking the steps three at a time, he burst through the door to the master bedroom.

Reuben lay on his side on the bed, leafing through a magazine. Tana stepped out of the bathroom, her face as white as the plastic bucket in her hand.

"Did you go outside?" Bolan said.

Tana nodded. "I didn't think they'd see.... They're out front. I'm sorry...."

Bolan pushed past her to the bathroom window. Three cars had parked on the gravel drive, and eight men with automatic weapons were exiting the vehicles. Bolan watched one of the men hold a walkie-talkie to his lips and speak.

The warrior hustled Tana and Reuben down the stairs, through the living room, to a sliding glass door leading to the back of the house. The front door opened as they exited onto a concrete porch.

The warrior led them past several fruit trees to the beach. They ducked around the corner of the next house in the row. "Stay here," he ordered.

Tana looked up at him, her face a mixture of fear and guilt. "I'm sorry," she said. "I didn't think—"

The Executioner shook his head. "There's no time for that now." He turned to Reuben. Yanking the Desert Eagle from the garbage bag, he handed it to the man. "They've got radios," he said. "I've got to neutralize these guys before more of them arrive. Stay put, and don't fire unless you have to."

The DEA agent nodded.

Bolan drew the Beretta and twisted the suppressor, satisfying himself that it was firmly screwed down. He crouched low, almost on all fours as he made his way back through the trees to the rear of the house.

A soft click from the sliding door pierced the silence as the Executioner took up position, his back pressed against the cold brick of the house. A moment later the door slid open on its track.

A balding cartel gunner stuck his nose through the opening, followed by the barrel of an M-16.

Bolan circled an arm around the man's neck and yanked him onto the porch.

The assault rifle in the gunman's hands began to rise. The Executioner pressed the Beretta under the man's arm and pulled the trigger, the 93-R coughing out one deadly round.

Bolan dropped the man to the concrete and entered the house. From the downstairs bedroom he heard voices. Creeping silently across the carpet, he peered into the room.

Two men in cammies stood facing the window. The taller of the two raised a walkie-talkie to his lips. "They aren't here, Mr. Mariategui," he said in Spanish, "but they couldn't have gone far."

The Beretta spit again, and the man dropped to the floor.

The shorter man wore an O.D. drill instructor's cap. A Llama .45 rode in a basket-weave holster on his hip. He half turned toward the door, his eyes wide with confusion as they stared down at his fallen comrade. As he spotted Bolan in the doorway, his hand dropped to the holster.

The Executioner squeezed the trigger again, and the near-silent round streaked through the gunman's face, knocking the cap to the floor. The man toppled after it.

More voices came from upstairs. The warrior heard the static scratches of another radio as he mounted the steps. He was halfway up when a tall, portly man with a full beard came out of the smaller bedroom.

The man froze in his tracks.

Bolan sent a double-tap of silenced rounds into his chest. The M-16 dropped from the guy's hands, and he fell forward, tumbling down the stairs past the Executioner.

"What was that?" came a voice from the master bedroom.

The warrior dropped the partial mag from the Beretta and rammed a fresh load home. He vaulted to the top of the stairs and raced into the master bedroom.

The remaining four men turned to the door. Bolan fired a quick round into the chest of the cartel gunner closest to the door. The man sprawled backward, his arms flailing in the air as he struggled to keep his feet. Another round from the Beretta drove him to the floor.

Bolan dived forward, hitting the ground as .223 autofire screamed above his head. Rolling to his stomach, he drove two 9 mm hollowpoints through the neck of a man wearing a camouflage boonie hat.

The warrior rolled to his side as a cartel gunner with an acne-scarred face raised his assault rifle. A 3-round burst from the Beretta sent the weapon flying from his grip, unfired.

The last man screamed, leapt over the bodies and raced for the door. The Executioner tapped the trigger, and another hollowpoint burst through the back of the fleeing man's neck, exiting through his cheek in a flurry of blood and teeth.

Static jumped from a walkie-talkie on the floor in the sudden silence. Then an unseen voice said, "Alfredo? Are you there?"

Bolan lifted the radio to his mouth. He hadn't heard any of the men speak enough to imitate a voice, but he had no choice. And it was worth a try.

The Executioner keyed the mike. "Yes," he said in Spanish. "Where are *you?*"

"A half mile away," the voice returned. "We'll be there in two minutes. Have you found them?"

Bolan pressed the button again. "No," he said. "False alarm. They're not here."

A long pause, then the voice said, "Alfredo? This isn't . . . who is this?"

Bolan bent down and grabbed an M-16 from the floor. He stuffed the walkie-talkie into his waistband and raced back down the steps, stopping on the back porch long enough to slide three extra .223 mags from pouches on the bald man's belt.

Sprinting back through the fruit trees to Reuben and Tana, he dropped the new weapon and walkie-talkie into the garbage bag. "Let's go," he said. "We've got less than two minutes before all hell breaks loose."

8

As they neared Rum Point, the outline of a parasail took shape in the sky above the sea. Then yellow hair and a bright red bikini stood out against the white clouds floating slowly toward the island. Two hundred feet of rope stretched tautly through the sky, coupling the woman to the ski boat below like a giant umbilical chord.

"Just where are we heading?" Tana asked as they hurried past a two-man catamaran moored a few feet out in the water.

"There's bound to be a dive shop up here," Bolan replied. "You and Reuben know how to dive. At this point it's our safest bet."

"But I told you... I've never been out of the swimming pool."

They passed a thatch-roofed gazebo bar. A bartender within the portable structure glanced quickly up, then returned his attention to the glasses in his hands.

Bolan patted Tana on the shoulder. "Open water's no different than a pool. It's just bigger."

"But couldn't we get lost?" she asked.

"Not if you stay with me. And if I have to, I'll tie you to me."

Tana grinned nervously.

Bolan led the Gonzalezes through the throng of people on the beach, careful to make sure the weapons were still hidden in the plastic trash bags.

As they neared the tip of the island, he saw a sign announcing Peter Cord's Dive Shop. A small grove of palms surrounded a parking lot to the rear of the shop, which opened onto the highway. A well-worn footpath led from the beachfront door to a small inlet from the sea.

Leaving Reuben and Tana at a beach table, the Executioner entered the shop. A tall, wiry man in his early thirties sat on a tall stool behind a glass counter. Remnants of muscle still hung around his bare chest and shoulders, but the abdomen had long ago softened and given in to flab. He glanced up, raising a glass of tomato juice into the air as Bolan entered the shop.

The Executioner nodded, scanning the room as he crossed to the counter.

"You Pete?"

"I be Pete," he drawled in a Southern U.S. accent.

"Need enough equipment for three."

Pete took another gulp of his juice. "Got any of your own stuff?"

"Not this time."

Bolan watched while Pete set his glass on the counter. Pointing to the side of his head, he grimaced and said, "Moving a little slow this morning—hell of a conch." He rose painfully from his stool, then squatted behind the counter. Bolan heard a cabinet slide open.

He glanced through the door to the beach, then out the window facing the highway. Still clear. He leaned over the counter. "Hate to hurry you," he said, "but we're on a tight schedule."

Pete had begun piling fins, rubber boots and masks with attached snorkels on the counter. He glanced up, then increased his speed slightly.

"We'll need six tanks and double harnesses."

Pete looked up over the countertop. "Planning to be out awhile?"

Bolan nodded. "Three BCD buoyancy units," he continued as the man rose to his feet and moved toward the wall. "Extra large, medium and small. And we'll all want power inflators running from the depth-pressure consoles on the regulators."

The warrior continued to scan the door and windows as Pete moved around the room, locating the gear and stacking it next to the door. He piled three diving knives on the counter. "Anything else?"

"I want emergency octopuses on each pack."

Pete nodded and tossed three orange-hosed regulators on the counter next to the knives.

Bolan's eyes fell on a large net and game-carry bag hanging from a hook on the wall. They were usually used by "buggers"—divers who hunted the shallow reefs for crab. He thought of the Desert Eagle, Beretta, M-16 and the All Terrain Chopper hidden in the trash bags. The thin plastic would last about thirty seconds underwater unless it was reinforced with something stronger. "I'll take that, too," he said, pointing to the bag.

Pete dropped it on the counter and began ringing up the charges on a scarred wooden cash register. He grinned widely as he worked. "You're about to make my hangover go away," he drawled. "May even take the old lady out tonight." He finished punching the keys, tore the receipt from the register and handed it to Bolan. "Three-oh-five. That's U.S. Hell, make it an even three hundred. Now, all I need is the bread and your certification cards."

Bolan pulled five hundred-dollar bills from his jeans and set them on the counter.

Pete frowned at the money, then looked up. "I need three C-cards," he said.

"Left them back in the room." Bolan pulled another bill from his pocket. "Try three C-*notes* instead."

"Hey, listen, buddy." His eyes darted from Bolan to the door, then back to the money on the glass in front of him. "It's my ass if I get caught, here."

Bolan didn't answer.

Pete continued to stare at the bills. "On the other hand, you *did* know your equipment." He paused again, then in one swift movement swept the money from the counter and stuffed it in his pocket. "Have a great dive."

Bolan, Reuben and Tana carried the equipment to the water. The Executioner left the weapons hidden in the trash bags and dumped them into the game net. He turned, watching the parking lot as he began assembling the hoses, gauges and other equipment.

He hadn't been able to listen to the walkie-talkie along the beach or in the dive shop, but he didn't need it to know cartel reinforcements would have arrived at the Melkas' house several minutes ago. After an initial inspection of the scene, they'd spread out, combing the beach and the road.

It would be only a matter of minutes before they'd arrive at Rum Point.

The Executioner had to get Reuben and Tana out of sight, underwater, before that happened. If Mariategui or any of the others saw them go under, it would literally be like shooting fish in a barrel.

Bolan watched Reuben hook the power-inflator line to his buoyancy unit. The man checked the connections, then twisted the valve on his tank, holding the regulator to his face and breathing. Tana was busily checking her gauges.

The Executioner relaxed slightly. They both seemed to have at least a rudimentary knowledge of what they were doing.

Bolan finished assembling his gear, pulled the black fins over his ankle-high rubber boots and tapped the power-inflator button, shooting air into the backpack. He lifted the tank harness in one hand and the game net in the other. Walking backward in the cumbersome fins into the incoming surf, he let the buoyancy unit float the tanks and slipped into the straps underwater.

Reuben and Tana joined him, pulling the masks over their faces and sticking their regulators into their mouths. They glanced at each other briefly, then dropped beneath the water.

Bolan dipped his mask into the water, wetting the inside to stop the fogging, then slipped it on.

As his head descended beneath the incoming waves, he saw three cars arrive in the parking lot of the dive shop.

One was a Ford, another was the green Plymouth.

The third was the cream-colored sedan.

MARIATEGUI STEPPED OUT of the long sedan. Several of the men had already entered the house. One man he didn't recognize held the front door open as he climbed the porch.

"You won't be pleased, boss," the man warned as his superior stepped through the opening.

Mariategui walked swiftly through the living room to the stairs. There, at the foot of the steps, lay the corpse of a man he knew only as Frederico. He glanced into the small bedroom to the side.

Mario and Antonio. Brothers from Cuzco.

He climbed the steps and met two more of his men coming out of another bedroom. They dropped their gazes to the floor as he stepped into the hallway. One of the men, short and thick, wore a red bandanna around his head. He nodded toward the open door. "Four more," he whispered.

From downstairs Mariategui heard the voice of his chauffeur. "José is in the back."

"Dead?" Mariategui called down the stairs.

"Dead."

The cartel man leaned through the door to the master bedroom. Littering the floor, he saw four lifeless bodies.

Mariategui felt no compassion, only contempt for these men, fools that they had been. Eight trained gunmen had fallen to the hands of two men and a woman.

They deserved their fate.

He stepped over the bodies and gazed out the window to the cars parked below. He pictured Hector Pizarro, alone in his office, the fat man's hands clasped behind his back as he watched his beloved piranhas devour goldfish.

The underboss's hand rose nervously to toy with the scar on his face. The fire spread quickly through his stomach. He glanced back to the corpses on the floor. Yes, these men had gotten just rewards for their stupidity.

But that didn't change the facts in regard to his *own* future—which would be short unless Cha-cha was found soon.

Mariategui moved back to the top of the stairs and called down the steps, "Lucaso, assemble the men."

He stood motionless as twenty armed gunmen crowded below. "Lucaso, take ten men and follow the beach to Rum Point," he ordered. "Carlos, take four and return across the swamp leading south."

A low groan came from below. Mariategui felt the anger race through his viens. Slowly he descended the stairs and walked toward a tall, angular man with a Fu Manchu mustache. "You aren't pleased with my orders, Carlos?"

Carlos averted his gaze and remained silent.

Mariategui reached under his silk jacket and jerked the nickel-plated Colt from his belt. He worked the slide with the thumb and forefinger of his left hand, jacking a round into the chamber.

Carlos glanced at him briefly, "I'm sorry, boss. I didn't mean to—"

Mariategui extended his arm, pressing the muzzle of the Colt into the man's forehead. Smiling, he pulled the trigger.

The shot thundered against the walls of the house.

The underboss turned to the other men, whose mouths hung open in shock. "Is there anyone else displeased with their assignment?" he asked softly.

No one spoke.

He shoved the gun back in his belt. "Juan," he continued, looking toward a man wearing an O.D. T-shirt. "You and Ramon will accompany me along the road."

"Yes, sir," a man in ragged slacks said eagerly.

Mariategui turned toward the men in general. "Now, we must all hurry. They can't have gotten far."

The words had no more than left his mouth when Mariategui heard the sound of car engines in the driveway. He moved quickly to the door and saw two Cayman Island police cars grind to a halt on the gravel.

Mariategui watched as a tall, thick-shouldered black man stepped from the lead vehicle. Two more officers, both white, exited the car to his rear.

The burly black man carried a shotgun. Neither of the other men was armed.

Mariategui moved back from the door, cursing under his breath. He had no time for trivial irritations. They had to move quickly, before Cha-cha and the others disappeared once more.

He heard the police officers' feet on the porch, and in that instant made his decision. The entire Cayman Island Police force numbered less than a hundred personnel, and that included many untrained clerical workers. There could be no more than forty active officers and investigators, and they were all novices when it came to weapons.

He, on the other hand, had a force close to twice that size. All were trained killers. He could destroy the entire Cayman Island police department. And he would. If need be, he'd lay siege to the whole island.

The big black man stepped through the door, the shotgun cradled in his arms. His mouth fell open as he tried to take in the situation he saw before him.

One of the cartel gunners drew back the bolt of his M-16, letting it slide forward hollowly in the silence. The other two police officers behind the black man stopped in their tracks and stared dumbly around the room.

The gunner with the M-16 glanced toward Mariategui. The underboss nodded, and the cartel man moved to the black cop's side, lifting the shotgun from his arms.

Mariategui walked forward slowly, his nickel-plated Colt dangling at the end of his arm. "You've chose an unfortunate moment for your visit," he said, smiling as he raised his weapon. He noticed the officer's name tag on his shirt. Bodden. A common name on the island.

But in a moment there'd be one less Bodden on Grand Cayman.

Captain Bodden's eyes closed as Mariategui pressed the pistol against his head and squeezed the trigger. Blood shot from the back of the man's head, then he fell to the floor next to Carlos.

The other two officers turned, bolting for the door. The cartel hitter with the M-16 dropped the first, sending a steady stream of autofire through his back.

Mariategui fired again, landing a 9 mm round between the shoulder blades of the second.

The cartel underboss turned back to his troops. "Let's go," he said, and led them through the door.

He slid into the back seat as his chauffeur jumped behind the wheel. Two more cars fell in behind. They drove quickly down the highway toward Rum Point, scanning the sides of the road as they went.

The cartel man directed his chauffeur into the parking lot of a scuba shop at the tip of the point. He got out of the sedan and stood beside the car, cupping a hand over his eyes to scan the beach.

Below, along the sand, he saw the usual sunbathers. Several yards out in the water, he watched as a scuba diver dropped below the water. Air bubbles appeared along the surface where his head had been.

Somewhere in the area Cha-cha, Tana and the mysterious American helping them had vanished. They were close. Mariategui could feel them.

He walked across the parking lot to the beach. A hundred yards along the sand, he saw an open-air gazebo bar. He strolled through the sunbathers and took a seat at the bar.

"What'll it be?" the bartender asked.

"Cuba libre." Mariategui watched as the man poured Jamaican rum into a tall glass and added ice and cola.

"I'm looking for three friends," he said when the bartender set the drink before him. "A Latino like myself, accompanied by a short, blonde American woman." He paused. "And another man. Have you seen them?"

The bartender rested his elbows on the counter and squinted into the bright sunlight off the beach. "The other man—big guy?" he asked.

"Yes, I believe so."

The bartender nodded. "Came along about fifteen minutes ago, I think. I mean, don't hold me to it. There's a lot of people out here." He waved a hand toward the beach, then reached below the bar for a towel. "Looked like they were in a hurry. I mean, if it *was* them."

Mariategui felt his pulse quicken. "Yes, they would have been in a hurry. Where did they go?"

The bartender shrugged and began wiping the counter. "Can't be sure. Like I said, lots of people out here." He smiled. "But wait a minute. Seems like I saw the couple sitting over next to the dive shop." He pointed toward a lot where the sedan was still parked. "Don't know where the big guy went. You might check with Pete, in there." The bartender laughed, straightened up and dropped the towel behind the bar. "That is, if you can catch him sober enough to remember."

Mariategui dropped a ten-dollar bill on the counter, got to his feet and walked toward the dive shop. His hand moved along his belt line, feeling the heavy Colt hidden beneath his silk coat.

He would catch this "Pete" sober, all right. And if he didn't, Marino Mariategui knew how to chase the haziness from his brain very quickly.

A SCHOOL OF PARROT FISH swam forward, then darted to the sides, passing the strange underwater intruders as Bolan led the Gonzalezes away from shore. Dragging the game net behind him, he stayed twenty feet below the surface as they flipped quietly over the yellow coral formations below. Thirty yards from the beach, the Executioner reached down, lifting the gauge console from the end of his line to check the compass.

He turned to Reuben and Tana. The woman's chest heaved in and out, sending an enormous mass of bubbles jetting from the sides of her regulator. Both the Gonzalezes raised their hands, forming *O* with thumbs and index fingers. Bolan nodded, returned the sign, then set course west around the point.

Keeping Reuben and Tana in sight at his sides, the Executioner tapped the power-inflation button, deflating his air pack slightly. Slowly he began to drift downward. When the gauge read fifty feet, he hit the other button on the inflator, achieved neutral buoyancy and floated motionless in the water as Reuben and Tana drifted down.

Bolan studied his bubbles as they drifted up to meet the descending couple. The tiny globes of air spread through the water, breaking long before they reached the surface. There was no need to turn this into a deep-sea dive, but he wanted to make sure they were sufficiently low enough that they didn't leave a telltale trail of bubbles everywhere they went.

Tana and Reuben joined him, flashing another "Okay" sign with their hands. Bolan turned and moved on through the open water.

He glanced back at the underwater shoreline in the distance. It was here that the decision had to be made. They could surface, then try to make it the rest of the way by either land or sea, but the cartel killers would still be close by. The risks would be reduced considerably if Tana and Reuben could make it all the way to Booby Cay.

Bolan stared through the water, studying Reuben's face through his mask. He appeared relaxed, almost tranquil. That could be either good *or* bad under the circumstances. The symptoms of his head injury might be evaporating.

Or they might have reappeared, combining with the new stress and the underwater atmospheric pressure to make him giddy.

Bolan got his attention, then raised his hand in front of the man's face. Quickly he flashed three fingers, one, then four and three again.

Reuben nodded, extended his hand and repeated the numbers in correct sequence.

Bolan reached out, grasping the line and hauling in the DEA man's dangling console. He stared at the pressure gauge. Not bad. Reuben's lungs were smaller. He'd used even less air than the Executioner.

The warrior watched Tana through the hard plastic of her mask. The woman's eyes were bloodshot, strained, worried, as she blew water through the nose valve. Bolan checked her gauge and felt his face tighten behind the face mask.

Tana couldn't have weighed more than ninety-five pounds, yet she was using more air than he or Reuben, the result of the deep, anxious breaths she'd been taking.

He'd have to watch her closely during the rest of the dive.

The Executioner led them west, following the coast around Water Point, then south again, along the edge of the sound. They came to a long line of coral arches reaching almost to the surface, and dropped lower, just below a hundred feet as they passed through the formations. They flipped slowly, steadily along beneath the sea, the Executioner keeping the pace easy to conserve air.

More parrot fish and sergeant majors joined their convoy as they passed over staghorn coral and neared the rotting remains of a sunken rowboat. Bolan stopped them again, checked Tana's gauge and switched her to her auxilary tank.

As they neared a coral mound alive with pulsating sponges, Bolan saw a sudden flurry of movement to his side. He turned to see Tana pull the regulator from her mouth and shake it violently. She shoved it back between her lips and reached frantically rearward to her tank valve.

The air bubbles shooting from her lips slowed, then halted abruptly.

Bolan flipped toward her, shaking his head and holding up a hand to tell her to stop, wait, he'd take care of it.

On the other side Reuben swam in her direction.

The terrified woman didn't see either one of them. She jabbed down on the power-inflator button with her thumb. Nothing happened. She frantically drew the knife from the rubber sheath on her leg. Slicing through the tank straps, she shot toward the surface as the empty tanks descended.

Bolan dropped the game net and hit his own button. His jaw tightened, and he felt the pressure building in his ears as he darted up through the water after Tana. He had to reach her, stop her before she ascended too quickly and developed an air embolism.

The Executioner swallowed hard, then cleared his throat as the force on his face, his ears, threatened to explode. He checked the depth gauge as he kicked furiously after Tana.

Seconds later Bolan felt a fin hit his outstretched hand. He kicked harder, reaching up through the flurry of movement overhead. His fingers brushed skin, and he circled them around Tana's ankle, jerking violently downward.

The woman bobbed down in the water, and Bolan grabbed his inflator control, tapping the button and jetting air from his vest. Achieving neutral buoyancy, the warrior tapped again on both buttons and they began to slowly descend.

Tana flailed furiously in the water, punching, kicking. Her hands found his head and ripped the mask from his face.

Staring blurry eyed through the saltwater, Bolan grabbed his emergency regulator—the octopus—from the snap on his buoyancy unit. Grabbing a handful of the woman's short blond hair in one hand, he steadied her head and shoved the octopus into the woman's mouth. He held on to her hair, encircling her shoulders with his other arm and pinning the hysterical woman's struggling arms to her sides.

He pressed his face against her mask. Breathe, he mouthed through the clear plastic.

A flicker of recognition shone suddenly in Tana's eyes. She bit down on the new regulator, breathed in, and slowly the fear began to leave her face.

Bolan found his mask at the end of the safety strap and shoved it back over his eyes. Tapping the drainage valve, he blew the water out as Tana continued to catch her breath.

Reuben arrived on her other side and grasped an arm. A mixture of horror and confusion radiated from the DEA man's eyes behind his own mask.

Tana closed her eyed briefly, then opened them. She held up a hand and circled her index finger into her thumb again.

With Reuben on one arm and the Executioner holding the other, they dropped slowly back to the bottom. Bolan lifted the game net with the weapons, and they started through the water once more.

TEN FEET ABOVE Reuben's head, the dark, steep bank rose to the surface. The DEA man felt Tana link her arm through his as Belasko ascended the rest of the way to the top.

Through vague eyes, Reuben watched the big man's head break through to the air. Belasko spun a quick three-sixty, searching the area, then his hand dipped down, motioning them up.

Reuben reached for his inflation valve, hit the wrong button, and they began to descend. He felt Tana's arm tighten around his. She reached around his waist, found the right button, and air shot into his buoyancy unit, dragging them to the top.

Reuben felt the sun burst on his face as he broke the surface. He turned, as if through a heavy fog, saw Tana pull his emergency octopus from her mouth. She smiled weakly, then turned to face the shore.

Belasko had already crawled onto the small marsh island he'd called Booby Cay. "How are you feeling?" he asked the agent.

Reuben forced a grin. "Not bad." He slid out of the tank harness and pushed them toward land. The tanks hit the edge, then slid back down the bank through the mud. "Shlippery." Reuben paused, aware that he'd slurred the word like a drunk.

Tana grabbed the tanks on the other side. Together they forced them onto the shore, then climbed on up.

"Take a breather," Bolan said. He began collecting their scuba equipment.

The DEA man stretched out next to his wife, cupping a hand on her shoulder. She turned to him and smiled faintly. Placing her hand over his, she closed her eyes.

Overhead, Reuben heard Belasko carrying their equipment somewhere into hiding. He closed his own eyes to rest.

Behind the dark lids, he saw colors racing across his vision in no discernible shapes or patterns. He tried to think of Tana—soft, beautiful, and now safe.

No, not safe. On a muddy island. Killers still coming. Tana almost died. Out of air. My fault.

Reuben forced his eyelids open, and now the colors dashed across the sky, standing out in sharp contrast to the darkening sky and heavy gray clouds. He shook his head again. Pain shot through his skull, but the colors faded, slowed.

Reuben forced himself to his knees and rubbed his forehead. His hand came away streaked with blood. He readjusted the bandage.

Belasko returned from wherever he'd hidden their scuba gear. Reuben squinted through the sunlight. The big man still had the net bag. Why? Reuben's foggy brain scrambled for the answer. Oh, yeah. Guns inside. He felt his head bobbing up and down, nodding to himself stupidly, answering his own question.

In the big man's other hand, Reuben saw the air-filled buoyancy backpack he'd worn. Sharp, searing pain shot through his brain as he concentrated, trying to figure out why Belasko hadn't hidden that with the other gear.

Belasko looked from Reuben to Tana, then back to Reuben. Behind the big American's deadpan expression, the DEA agent saw the concern in his eyes. Belasko had caught him in his mindless reverie.

"Ready?" the big man asked.

Reuben nodded. He had to hide the extent of his injury from this man. For Tana's sake. If Belasko realized how bad his head really was, he might stop wherever they were and seek medical help. More danger for Tana.

Tana stood, then leaned down and helped him to his feet. Arm in arm, they followed Bolan across another marsh swamp to the other side of the small offshore island.

The Warrior stopped at the edge of the water and pulled a thin cord from his buttpack. He tied the handle of the net bag to the air-filled buoyancy unit, then dropped them both into the water.

"You and Tana hang on to the sides."

Reuben felt the cool water again as he slid from the shore. He grasped the side of the bobbing canvas air bladder.

Tana did the same on the other side, taking a few seconds to rub some of the mud from her arms.

Bolan positioned himself in front of them. Reaching back to grab one of the straps, he began side-stroking through the water, towing them.

Reuben tried to kick, but his legs each seemed to be on different wavelengths from his brain. They fluttered ineffectively beneath the surface.

Reaching the shore, the big man dragged the bag and backpack over the side and hid the buoyancy unit behind a mangrove. He opened the net and removed an M-16. Next came his handguns, and then the big man was handing Reuben his own SIG-Sauer.

With Belasko in the lead, they made their way along the coast, trudging through the mud. Reuben moved along behind him, Tana on his arm. Sharp, shooting pains alternated with a dull, distant pounding in his skull.

The sky continued to darken overhead. Belasko finally stopped, pointing in the distance. Reuben squinted through the pain, forcing his eyes to focus hazily on a long, man-made channel cut into the shore in the distance.

Rows of houses lined both banks. Small private piers ran the channel, one at the rear of each house. And docked at many of the piers were boats. Boats, piers, and houses seemed to sway on the water as Reuben struggled to watch.

"You two wait here." Belasko's voice sounded far away. "I'll get us a ride on in. Lay down. Rest some more, Reuben." The big man pointed again, this time toward a clump of mangroves near the shore. To Reuben the movement appeared to be done in slow motion, like the instant replay of a knockout punch in a boxing match.

With the same slow motion, Belasko handed Reuben the M-16.

The DEA man and his wife moved to the trees, taking seats in the mud. He watched as Belasko crept quickly along the shore toward the boats.

Then Reuben Gonzalez felt his head slap wetly into the mud. Somewhere in the distance he heard his wife's voice. "Honey? Honey?"

She sounded frightened again. Reuben tried to answer, put her at ease, remind her that everything would be all right—Belasko would take care of it. He felt his lips move, heard unintelligible utterances. His eyes closed.

He'd answer her later, he promised himself. Like Belasko had said, it was time to rest some more.

The pain in his head softened, and the nausea disappeared.

Reuben's last thought was how cool the mud felt against his cheek.

9

Wind whipped through Bolan's hair as he twisted the steering wheel, guiding the sixteen-foot powerboat across the quickly rising waves of North Sound. Spiky sprays of saltwater stung his skin, blasting like sand into the open wounds left by tree branches, jungle vines and mosquitoes.

He glanced quickly over his shoulder. Tana sat behind him, Reuben's head in her lap. The woman's eyes reflected her fear.

Bolan glanced toward the mouth of the sound. The heavy prestorm waves of the Caribbean compressed as they left the sea to crash through the boundaries of the sound, then rose high in the air to compensate for the narrower passageway.

The warrior knew Tana feared the rough water, but the majority of her fright came from her husband's sudden relapse. He glanced again over his shoulder.

Reuben was awake, but only in a sense. He smiled idly up at the dark sky like an infant, with no conception of the danger presented by the rising swells.

The DEA agent had been unconscious when Bolan returned with the boat. Tana had been shaking him roughly by the shoulders, slapping his face, frantically trying to revive him.

Smelling salts from the Executioner's first-aid kit had done the trick, but Reuben had stumbled once they got him to his feet, then fallen again twice on the way to the boat. Bolan had finally carried him through the marsh to the water, eased him over the edge of the craft and strapped him into the seat.

Reuben hadn't spoken since or moved on his own power.

Black clouds hurried across the sky as the Executioner pushed onward across the water. Another massive wave neared the boat from the mouth of the sound, its whitecapped crest sparkling under the fading sunlight.

Bolan twisted the steering wheel, meeting the wall of water head-on. The bow of the boat nosed upward, then plummeted again as the wave passed under them.

The warrior turned back toward the southern coast in the distance, his eyes scanning both the water and shore for any signs of the cartel. The few boats on the sea had quickly deserted when the waters turned hellish, the fishermen not anxious to risk their lives for another wahoo or bonefish.

The shore appeared deserted, as well, natives and tourists alike finding refuge to ride out the oncoming storm.

A light mist began to fall. A moment later thunder cracked stunningly overhead, and sheets of rain drenched them.

Bolan wiped the water from his face with the back of his arm. He stared through the darkening skies. Far in the distance he saw the sign—MacLivish Gardens.

The shape of the stone jetty took form, and he changed course slightly, heading toward the shore. He'd seen the Gardens on the map—another small housing development. It was the closest he could get them to the airport without drawing attention.

And a likely place to appropriate land transport.

He slowed the boat as they neared the shore, scanning the coastline once more for signs of gunmen. Nothing. Cutting the engine, he let the vessel bounce through the water toward the pier.

A wave caught the stern, driving the bow hard into the wooden dock. Bolan leapt onto the pier, grasped the line and wrapped it around a metal cleat embedded in the wood.

He turned to Tana and extended his arm. "Come on. Quickly."

She didn't move.

Bolan reached back, grabbing her roughly by the shoulder. With Reuben in the middle of a relapse from his injuries, it was no time for his wife to slip back into her semicatatonic dream state.

He shook her again, then tapped lightly on her cheek. "Snap out of it, Tana. Reuben and I need your help."

Slowly the film lifted from the woman's eyes.

Bolan pulled her onto the dock, then dropped back into the boat. He draped the battle harness over his shoulder, slung the M-16 across his back and hefted Reuben over his shoulder. Carrying the DEA man, the Executioner hurried up the concrete steps that led to the housing development, Tana at his heels.

An '83 Oldsmobile two-door had been parked by the side of the closest house. Rain continued to hammer against the back of their necks as they raced toward it.

Bolan left them at the house behind the car. "Wait here," he ordered.

Tana nodded. Reuben grinned silently into space.

The warrior clutched the car door and pulled, his wet fingers sliding off the handle as more thunder rumbled in the blackened skies. Locked.

He scanned up and down the tract of houses. The only other vehicle in sight was a Volkswagen Beetle parked a hundred yards away.

Too slow, and too far away.

Drawing the big Desert Eagle from his waistband, Bolan rammed it through the Olds's driver-side window. He opened the door, dropped the M-16 on the seat, slid across the broken glass and ducked under the dashboard.

As his fingers searched for the appropriate wires, the Executioner heard a car engine nearing. The vehicle halted somewhere to the rear of the Olds. He paused, his ears probing for clues as to who might be behind the wheel.

Then the soft patter of tiny feet on the mud echoed through the wind, and Tana's running form passed by the broken window toward the rear of the Olds.

"Please!" Bolan heard her scream through the rain. "Give us a ride! My husband . . ."

The warrior rose slightly, peering over the back seat. Through the rear window, he saw three men exit a pale blue Cutlass. One man, wearing a yellow rain slicker, held a walkie-talkie in his hand. All three squinted through the downpour, their expressions turning to grins as their hands reached under their rain gear.

Bolan slid the M-16 from the plastic garbage bag and flipped the safety as the men drew weapons. The man in the yellow slicker moved quickly around the Olds, training his own M-16 on Reuben.

A cartel gunner wearing a light nylon windbreaker lunged suddenly forward, his arm circling around Tana's neck in a headlock. He pressed the muzzle of a Llama Small Frame automatic against her temple.

The Executioner rested the assault rifle over the seat, dropping the front sight on the forehead of the man in the windbreaker. His target was less than a foot above Tana's own head. It would be a close shot, but he didn't have time to wait for a better one.

The Executioner squeezed the trigger. A steady stream of rounds shattered the rear windshield, continued through the glass and struck the man in the face and throat. Blood poured from the wounds, splashing against Tana as the man with the Llama fell to the ground.

Bolan twisted in the seat. A second burst of fire blew the front windshield from the Oldsmobile and took out the man in the slicker. The M-16 dropped from his hands, and the cartel killer fell forward over Reuben's lap.

The third man gaped awkwardly at his fallen comrades. Bolan turned the M-16 his way, a 3-round burst taking him out.

The Executioner heard more car engines in the distance. He turned back to Tana.

"Get in the car!" he shouted above the thunder.

She ran forward.

Bolan jumped from the Olds and sprinted to where Reuben still sat expressionless, the man in the slicker stretched across his legs. Throwing the corpse to the side, the Executioner grabbed Reuben under the arms, hauled him to the back seat of the Olds, opened the door and laid him across the seat. Tana jumped in next to her husband. The warrior jammed the wires together and the Olds roared to life. Tana remained silent, aware of her grave error.

The Executioner threw the Olds into Drive, the car sliding as it took off down a winding street. He glanced at Tana in the rearview mirror. He liked the woman. She and her husband were both doing their best, working within their respective limitations. A reprimand wasn't going to do her, her husband, or Bolan himself, any good.

Bolan came to a fork in the road and veered to the right, instinct telling him they were turning toward the airport. Rain and wind blustered through the shattered window and both windshields as he floored the accelerator.

Ahead Bolan spotted the highway leading to the airport.

At the same time, he saw six cars. The cream-colored sedan was in the middle of the pack, waiting to turn into the housing area.

THUNDER, LIGHTNING, and rain cut through the airwaves, making the walkie-talkie crackle with static. Each time it squeaked, Mariategui flinched, as if someone had scratched the length of a chalk board with their fingernails.

"Boss." A voice suddenly sounded through the dissonance. "We've found Cha-cha and his wife."

"Your location?"

A short pause while the static returned. Then, "We're nearing a small dock at MacLivish Gardens." More static. "The housing development is right next to the airport."

Mariategui sat back against the cushion in the back seat. Lowering the walkie-talkie's volume he watched two of the cartel's rented vehicles pull out in front of his car. His chauffeur fell in behind, and they started along the blacktop leading to the highway.

The underboss held the radio to his lips. "Where's the other man?"

"We don't know, but he must be close by."

"Kill *him*, if you must," Mariategui instructed, "but don't kill Cha-cha. He's mine."

He drew his Colt and set it on his lap. Pulling a long brown Cuban cigar from the breast pocket of his silk jacket, he jammed it between his teeth as the driver neared the intersection with the highway.

So this was where the White Ghost had led them.

Mariategui felt himself grinning around the cigar as he leaned forward, pressing the lighter in the back of the seat. He traced up and down the scar on his face as he waited for the lighter to heat.

Until they rented the scuba gear, their plan had obviously been to contact a fourth confederate on the island. Each place they'd stopped, they'd used the phone.

But something had gone wrong. Whoever had been waiting to pick them up was no longer there. Perhaps one of the cartel's own men had killed him. Not that it mattered.

What mattered was that it had forced Cha-cha and his confederates to change their plan. And as soon as the drunken scuba pro had realized he would live longer if he cooperated, Mariategui had known what that plan had to be.

The lighter popped out, and Mariategui held it to the end of his cigar. The pain in his belly had vanished.

He drew the smoke deep into his lungs, luxuriating in the pleasure his ulcer usually prohibited. And as soon as he put a bullet between the eyes of the traitor, he'd feel better yet.

Mariategui replaced the lighter and took another draw from the cigar, letting the deep, aromatic smoke roll around his tongue before it drifted from his mouth and nose. He'd known immediately that they could never reach the airport underwater. It was simply too far. They'd have to surface somewhere and return to land or find a boat. But regardless of the route they chose, they'd eventually end up at the airport.

So it was to the airport he'd gone, and with him, the bulk of his troops.

The driver continued down the highway as the rain drilled down on the roof of the sedan. Mariategui thought of the uncomfortable police and customs officials back at the terminal. They knew what was happening—there was no way for them not to. But they also knew they were outnumbered and out-

gunned. And by now word of the deaths of three police officers would have spread throughout the island.

The Cayman Island police had reacted prudently to
the arrival of Mariategui's army at the airport. They'd
ignored them.

The underboss inhaled another pull of the rich cigar smoke. The pain in his abdomen flickered for a
moment.

They still didn't have the big American's location.

Then the pain went away as he realized it made no
difference. Cha-cha was the important one. They'd
find this White Ghost soon enough. He had to be
nearby.

The sedan slowed as they neared the entrance to
MacLivish Gardens. Mariategui leaned to one side of
the driver, watching through the windshield as the lead
car in the procession waited for a vehicle in the oncoming lane to pass.

From the housing development road, an Oldsmobile slowed at the intersection, then turned right. At
the same time, the cartel underboss saw his lead car hit
its brakes and come to a halt.

Static from the radio screeched once more in his
ears, then an excited voice said, "Sir! The car turning
toward you...it's them!"

Mariategui felt the cigar drop from his mouth. He
reached for the Colt with one hand, furiously rolling
down the window with his other. He thumbed the
hammer, then jammed the weapon through the window.

But by then the Oldsmobile had passed.

BOLAN TAPPED THE BRAKES as the first car turned into the housing development. "Duck down," he ordered Tana.

The woman hesitated, then dropped below the back seat as the first car, a dark-colored Toyota, drew abreast.

Through the pounding rain the Executioner saw the startled expression on the driver's face. The man jerked a walkie-talkie toward his mouth.

He'd seen her.

The warrior turned right, straining to catch the expression on the face of the second car's driver. Nothing.

Glancing in the rearview mirror, he saw the brake lights glowing through the downpour as the Toyota stopped abruptly, just past the entrance.

The Oldsmobile picked up speed. Bolan studied the third car in the convoy—the cream-colored sedan—Mariategui's. The passenger's seat was vacant. Then, as they passed, he saw the cartel man's face snap against the window in the back seat.

Bolan floored the accelerator.

The Executioner stared into the mirror. Behind him the Toyota was backing out of the house next to the road. The other four cars screeched through U-turns on the highway.

Tana sat back up again.

"Get back down," Bolan told her. "Get Reuben on the floor, too. It's not over yet."

Rain poured through the blown-out windshields, soaking Bolan's clothes and impairing his vision. The Olds slowly gained speed as they pressed on toward the airport. Scattered shops and cafés began to appear through the downpour as they neared George Town. Here and there a tourist braved the rain, walking along the highway's narrow shoulder. But for the most part Grand Cayman's main thoroughfare remained deserted.

Bolan glanced down to the speedometer. They were nearing seventy, which was all he could handle on the slippery, twisting curves. A sign announcing Owen Roberts International Airport flew past on his right. One half mile.

Rounding another hairpin curve, the Executioner headed into a straightaway. Gazing into the mirror once more, he saw the pursuit vehicles round the curve a hundred yards behind, the cream-colored sedan leading the pack.

He kept high speed as he neared the airport, waiting until they were fifty yards from the turnoff to tap the brakes. As the Oldsmobile slowed, threatening to skid out of control across the slick pavement, he saw a Dodge pickup and a Chrysler LeBaron at the intersection.

The pickup bed was filled with men in fatigues, their M-16s pointing skyward.

Bolan's foot shot from the brakes, hitting the accelerator as the pickup jerked out onto the highway, foolishly trying to block him off. He saw the horror on the faces of the men in the back as, instead of slowing to a stop, the Olds increased speed.

Twisting the steering wheel at the last instant, Bolan let his vehicle glance off the left front fender of the

Dodge. The men in back flew over the rail, screaming as the pickup spun a full 360 degrees.

The Olds skidded briefly, fishtailing down the highway toward a car in the oncoming lane. From the back seat the Executioner heard Tana's shrill screams. He fought the wheel, working it with the brake, maneuvering the vehicle back across the yellow line a split second before a Plymouth Fury raced past.

The warrior pressed the accelerator again, gradually picking up speed as the chase cars quickly closed the gap. Racing on past the airport, they sped toward George Town.

The airport was no longer an option. So much for Plan A.

Bursts of automatic gunfire erupted from the rear. Bolan glanced into the side-view mirror, seeing the LeBaron, followed closely by Mariategui's sedan, nearing their bumper. Then the side mirror exploded into a thousand bits of glass.

The Executioner guided the Olds around several curves, pushing the sluggish car to eighty. The tires on the opposite side of each breathtaking turn left the ground twice, threatening to overturn them.

The shots from the pursuit vehicles stopped. The cartel gunners were evidently satisfied to wait until they reached the city and traffic forced their prey to a slower speed.

Bolan kept his foot firm on the pedal, fully aware that every second they lost slowing down would take ten to regain in the lethargic Olds.

He followed the highway as it bent north, away from the sea, circling the inland edge of the capital city. He rounded a final curve and hit the brakes behind a long line of jammed traffic.

Skidding to the right, the Executioner guided the Olds along the highway's shoulder. He ignored the squalling horns and angry curses of drivers as he skippered the car expertly around pedestrians diving for cover. Reaching the end of the traffic jam, he pulled back onto the road and slowed to the speed limit as the rain finally halted.

He drove carefully, checking the rearview mirror every few seconds for pursuit. None was visible. Mariategui and the others had either been slowed or halted by the long line of cars.

Bolan blew air from his lips. Each second took them farther away from the airport they'd fought so hard to reach. But that was out of the question now. The cartel had overrun the area. Even if they reached the terminal, they'd be shot down before they could find Grimaldi or make arrangements to get safely off the island.

No, they had one hope left. They had to find a place to hide out, someplace where he could place a call to Brognola to see if the officials of the Cayman Islands wanted to reconsider their refusal of American intervention.

Now that their island was being torn to shreds.

But just where was that place? Bolan wondered as they left George Town proper and headed north along the coast.

"Reuben's coming around," Tana said, her voice shaking.

"Keep him down," Bolan told her. "And *you* stay down with him. By now every cartel hardguy with a walkie-talkie's got a full description of this car. No telling when we'll run into more of them."

He scanned the road, looking for a place to ditch the car. He had mixed feelings. If he stopped to get Reuben and Tana out of the car, they'd be sitting ducks until they got to cover.

And if they continued north, they stood a good chance of running into whatever troops Mariategui had assigned to the West Bay area. They stood an even better chance of running out of island.

As they neared the Caribbean Club on Seven Mile Beach, shots sounded from the parking lot. Two rounds skimmed across the hood, altered course, then spiderwebbed patterns through what glass still remained in the passenger's window.

Bolan hit the gas. The Olds sputtered past the club as four more vehicles screeched onto the highway behind them.

More auto fire drilled into the back of the Olds. Bolan looked into the mirror to see a cammie-clad man with an M-16 hanging from the passenger window of a Trans Am. Three other vehicles brought up the rear.

From the back seat of the Oldsmobile came an unsteady voice. "Belasko, hand me a rifle..."

Bolan hesitated. The man's condition was indeterminable. Still, as a DEA Special Agent he'd spent thousands of hours on the firing range. Firing a weapon should be second nature to him.

Another burst of fire flew through the back and exited through the front of the open car. There was no way they'd outrun the Trans Am, not on the open road. And if one round found a crucial spot in the Olds...

The warrior reached down, grasped the barrel of the M-16 and pushed it over the seat. "Go for the tires."

Reuben rose slightly in the seat and rested the assault rifle on the rear dash, the barrel extending through the blown glass. Bolan heard him take a deep breath, a painful sigh erupting as he let the air out.

As they sailed past the Holiday Inn, Reuben squeezed the trigger.

Brass casings flew through the car, the hot metal landing on the Executioner's neck and shoulders. Bolan looked once more to the mirror and saw the Trans Am's left wheel suddenly dip.

The highly tuned car swerved into the oncoming lane, then fishtailed back. Bolan heard a crash, then the highpitched squeal of metal on metal screeched along the beach road as one of the other pursuit vehicles scraped off the Trans Am's rear.

Bolan pressed harder on the accelerator, gaining precious seconds as the remaining cartel vehicles slowed to avoid the wreck. As they passed the Galleon Beach hotel, he saw the Chevy and Subaru pass the crash site, then speed up as they gained open road.

The Olds passed the governor's mansion, then a small cemetery. Bolan felt the cool wind from the rain on his face as they neared West Bay. He had to get ahead, out of sight, then get the hell off the highway before it ended at the sea.

But the two pursuit vehicles were closing the gap with every heartbeat.

Reuben fired again. Nothing. Then the Executioner saw a flash of red as they passed a sign announcing Upper Land to the right. He wrenched the wheel toward the middle of the road, avoiding the crimson sight to his side, then heard the screech of tires.

As they flashed past the intersection, the Executioner saw a cherry-red two ton truck spin to a stop in the middle of the highway, temporarily blocking the road.

Bolan bore down on the pedal, rounded three more curves and entered the township of West Bay. A final glance into the rearview showed a clear highway behind.

Shortly he came to another small road paralleling the sea, turned south and saw a sign in front of several large tanks along the beach: Cayman Island Turtle Farm. Visitors Welcome.

He watched a brown Ford station wagon turn left into the parking lot. He slowed, then followed them in, pulling up alongside as a middle-aged man and woman stepped from the car. He exited the Olds and walked forward as the man, wearing a floral-print Hawaiian-style shirt, sunglasses and a straw hat, waited for the two bored-looking teenage girls to get out of the back seat. "Come on," the man urged, "it'll be fun."

Bolan tapped him on the shoulder, and the man turned around.

"I need to borrow your car."

"What? What the hell do you—" The man fell silent as his gaze dropped to where the Desert Eagle protruded from Bolan's belt. He drew in a deep breath. "Yes," he sputtered, "I was about to offer it. Anything for a fellow American."

"Good. Because I need your hat and sunglasses, too."

Slowly the man handed Bolan his car keys, then removed his hat and sunglasses.

The Executioner hurried back to the Olds. Together he and Tana helped Reuben to the rear of the station wagon and stretched him out across the seat. Tana crawled in behind her husband.

Bolan started the engine and glanced down at the gas gauge. Less than an eighth of a tank, but better than nothing.

The family of four stood gawking in the parking lot as they drove away.

The warrior steered the station wagon along the coast as night fell over the Caribbean. He continued to scan the highway as he drove. He had to find either a quick place to hide or a service station.

They'd be taking a hell of a chance stopping for gas, but the fresh wheels wouldn't be easily spotted by the cartel.

"Can I get up yet?" Tana asked.

"No. There's no point in taking chances."

The highway traffic was light. There was no sign of the Chevy or Subaru, and none of the few cars that passed on their way into West Bay looked suspicious.

But Mariategui and his horde of Lima Cartel gunmen hadn't evacuated the island. They weren't about to give up, not with a witness alive who could put all of them behind bars.

Just because Bolan couldn't see them didn't mean they weren't nearby. They were.

The Executioner could smell them.

10

Bolan scanned the beaches and side roads as he drove, searching for any place where Reuben and Tana might be safe while he called Brognola. But each location that looked as if it would have a phone also swarmed with tourists—tourists who might be cartel men in disguise.

And every spot deserted by people had no signs of a telephone.

As they neared George Town again, Bolan glanced at the gas gauge needle which had finally dropped to empty. He could postpone the inevitable no longer. He had to find a service station.

He finally spotted a tiny service station on the beach side of the highway. Far from any other buildings, it sat a hundred feet off the highway, alone amid a grove of swaying palms.

The Executioner turned onto the dirt road leading to the station, then pulled up to the lone pump. Without turning around, he said, "We're getting gas. Keep your heads down. I'll be right back."

"Okay," came the soft, frightened answer from the rear of the vehicle.

A toothless old man wearing a long-billed fisherman's cap and oil-stained khakis limped toward the station wagon. "Help ya?" he asked.

"Fill it. Unleaded."

"Damn good thing," the old man replied, his toothless lips flapping. "'Cause no-lead's all we got."

Taking a final glance around, the Executioner slid across the seat and got out on the passenger's side, closest to the office.

Inside the station a variety of Cayman Island T-shirts hung from nails along the wall. His white, cut-off sweatshirt practically dripped mud—a dead giveaway if cartel men spotted it.

He found three shirts, two navy blue and one black, bearing the likeness of Sir Turtle, the peg-legged mascot of the Islands. Dropping his sweatshirt into the wastebasket by the counter, he pulled the extralarge over his shoulders. With the medium and small under his arm, he walked back toward the car.

Bolan watched a Ford Bronco drive slowly by as he crossed to the station wagon. The driver was young, blond haired. It wasn't likely that he'd be with the Peruvians. Another shadowy figure was silhouetted next to him. The Executioner couldn't get a good look, but he got a *bad* feeling.

The old man stood next to the gas tank as he approached. The Warrior pulled some bills from his pocket and pressed them into the man's hand. "That'll be enough."

"But you said fill 'er. Just another—"

Bolan grabbed the old man by the shoulders and threw him to the ground next to the station wagon as the Bronco reappeared, the barrel of an M-16 extending through an open window.

Drawing the Desert Eagle from his waistband, the Executioner fired two shots through the windshield. The first caught the driver in the chest, and the man slumped forward. The second entered the top of the driver's blond head and traveled on, somewhere through the vehicle.

The Bronco continued forward, striking the pump, and gasoline sprayed across the lot. Bolan started to fire again as the darkskinned man in the passenger's seat pushed his blond partner through the driver's door to the ground.

No. Gasoline had soaked the entire area. He couldn't afford to risk another round igniting the pump.

The warrior ripped open the station wagon's door. Grabbing the toothless old man under the arms, he tossed him across the front seat as two more cartel vehicles screeched to a halt next to the Bronco.

Bolan dived behind the wheel and twisted the key. The station wagon screeched across the lot toward the dirt road, tearing the pump nozzle from the tank hole and ripping the hose in half. More gasoline spewed across the drive.

Three shots sounded behind them as the wagon turned onto the road. Then suddenly the night lit up like the fires of hell.

The stench of gasoline was thick in Bolan's nostrils as he turned back onto the highway. He watched as first the three cartel vehicles, then the entire service station, exploded and burst into flames.

The old man next to him dropped his toothless lower lip. He turned toward the Executioner, and the shock turned to a wide, floppy grin. "Been tryin' to unload the place for years," he commented. "No buyers."

Bolan floored the accelerator and raced toward George Town. "You have insurance, I take it."

"You betcha." The old man settled back, a look of pure contentment covering his face.

The warrior slowed as they reached George Town. He'd seen no signs of additional pursuit, but it was just a matter of time. The radio-equipped cartel vehicles would be racing to the scene, and it wouldn't take them long to find someone who'd witnessed the spectacle and seen the station wagon heading toward town.

They reached the city limits. The Executioner cut down a side street, passed the harbor, then another small cemetery. He turned the wagon toward a long row of churches.

He was looking for a place to drop his new passenger when the old man spoke again. Pointing toward a square building with a tall, spiraling steeple, he said, "I'll be gettin' out here, thank ye. Just in time for prayer meetin'."

Bolan pulled to the curb.

The old man stepped out of the car, then leaned back in. "Whoever ye might be, lad," he said, "I'll be thankin' you for yer help." He tossed the money Bolan had given him onto the seat. "This gas's on me."

Singing a tune the Executioner didn't recognize, he limped across the street toward the church.

Bolan continued down the street, then turned onto cracked blacktop bordering the sea. A thick forest of sea pines separated the road from the beach, the water peeking through the limbs at intervals as he drove through the residential area of the city. They passed signs announcing the Seaview Hotel, Sunset House and several large oil tanks. The Executioner drove on past the Casa Bertmar Hotel and Scuba Shop, then cut into a short drive leading to the sea.

Smith Cove.

The map had shown it as a small rocky inlet, used mainly by swimmers, sunbathers and scuba divers. Unless there was a night dive going on, it should be deserted.

He cut the lights as he turned, then the engine as he parked three feet from the water. Covering the M-16 with the torn remnants of the garbage bag, he opened the back door of the station wagon and helped Tana out onto the rocky shore.

"Reuben's unconscious again," she whispered.

Bolan looked down at her. Tears streamed from her eyes, and her frail shoulders hunched forward in defeat, making her look even smaller in the moonlight.

He placed a hand on her shoulder, then lifted her chin with his index finger. He didn't speak.

Tana fell forward, her arms circling his waist, her face pressed to his chest. Deep, heavy sobs sounded in the stillness.

The warrior let her cry, then gently pushed her to arm's length. "Tana," he said, "it's not over yet, but we're getting close. There's a light at the end of the tunnel. We're going to make it out of here, and Reuben will be fine. But again, he needs your help. I need your help.''

She looked up at him, and Bolan saw the trust in her face. Slowly she wiped her eyes with the back of her hand. ''Really?''

''You've got my word on it.''

Tana wiped her eyes again. ''What are we doing?''

''Reuben can't travel anymore. I'll find a place to hide the two of you, then ditch the car. I don't want it pointing the way for Mariategui. Then I'm going to find a phone and call a man I know in Washington.''

''Will he help?''

''He always has,'' Bolan replied.

The warrior lifted Reuben from the station wagon, Tana following as he carried the sleeping DEA agent over the craggy shore. Fifty yards south of the cove they came to another, smaller grotto cut into the jagged terrain. Millions of years of erosion had eaten several small cavities into the rocks, and Bolan set the unconscious man on the ground inside the largest. He felt himself frowning as he surveyed the area.

It wasn't a cave. Reuben and Tana wouldn't be totally hidden from sight if a cartel patrol came along the shore, but it was the best he could hope for on such short notice.

Reuben was fading fast. If he didn't get medical attention in the next few hours, Mariategui wouldn't have to lift a finger.

Tana dropped down, taking a seat next to Reuben under the low overhang. Bolan knelt in front of her, just outside the shallow eaves. He lifted her chin again and stared into her eyes. ''There's one more thing,

Tana,'' he said, ''and it's going to be hard for you. You're a kind, loving woman, and it'll go against your nature. It'll go against everything you've ever been taught. Everything you've believed up to this point in your life.''

The woman's eyes opened wider, but she didn't speak.

Bolan continued. ''Reuben's still got his weapon, but he's in no shape to use it. He might come around again while you're out here, and then again, he might not.'' The Executioner reached under his T-shirt, pulled the Beretta from his jeans and handed it to her, butt first.

Tana shook her head vigorously. ''No, Mr. Belasko, I can't—''

''If the cartel men find you, Tana, they'll kill you. And they'll kill Reuben. You understand that now, don't you?''

She nodded slowly.

''Then take it. If not for yourself, then for Reuben.''

The little woman reached up, her childlike fingers wrapping around the Beretta's grip.

Briefly Bolan explained the double-action mechanism. ''Don't worry about the safety. It's off, but the gun's still safe. Just aim it and pull the trigger. You'll have to pull hard the first time. The second pull will be easier.'' With a last pat of encouragement on her shoulder, the warrior turned away.

As he made his way back across the rugged shore to the station wagon, the Executioner wondered if the gentle young woman would be able to use the gun. He hoped it wouldn't come to that. But if it did, and Tana Gonzalez couldn't bring herself to pull the trigger, he'd never see either of the Gonzalezes alive again.

THE EXECUTIONER DREW the Desert Eagle and took cover behind the rocks. He scanned the isolated grotto in the darkness, listening for any sounds of humanity.

Satisfied that the station wagon hadn't been discovered, he crept from the rocks, slid behind the wheel and pulled back onto the highway.

Bolan turned away from the sea into the residential area. His eyes scanned the streets under the light posts, scrutinizing the area for a spot to ditch the Ford. Two blocks down he saw a grouping of buildings. Driving on, a basketball goal and soccer field came into focus.

A school. Just what he needed. If he left the station wagon in front of a house, Mariategui or other cartel members might spot it. The people who lived in the house—the whole neighborhood, for that matter—might find themselves suddenly at gunpoint, being asked questions to which they didn't know the answers.

The Executioner pulled the M-16 from under the garbage bag, wrapping the weapon once again. Tattered and torn, the sack would still break the assault rifle's distinctive outline in the darkness.

Leaving the keys in the ignition, he jogged back toward the sea, hidden in the shadows close to the houses. The sounds of approaching automobiles came down the quiet road as he neared the highway.

Ducking back behind the corner house, the Executioner watched as the cream-colored sedan, followed by another vehicle, slowly passed—Mariategui, going south toward Smith Cove.

Bolan hesitated. They were patrolling the road. Running across Reuben and Tana on the beach, in the short length of time he'd be gone, would be a long shot.

He waited until the taillights disappeared around a curve, then sprinted across the highway to the cover of the pines. He made his way through the trees to the beach.

No, if he went back now, they'd be no better off than before, scrambling from one brush with death to the next. And Reuben's flight was over. The brave little DEA agent had done his best, fought a good fight, but the pace was literally killing him.

Reaching the beach, the Executioner turned north. He had to push on, contact Brognola and return as quickly as possible. There was no other way.

Bolan broke into a jog, the soles of his deck shoes slapping wetly along the sand. He passed another area of iron shore and veered out into the water, avoiding the jagged rocks. He saw lights ahead, then heard muffled voices.

He cut back across the rocks to the tree line. Returning to the sand, he walked calmly toward the lights of the Casa Bertmar Hotel, passing several small cottages along the shore. A young man and woman, arm in arm, ignored him as they strolled along the beach.

A long wooden ramp led from the beach to the back porch of the hotel. A small building was set to one side, a hand-printed sign announcing it simply as the Dive Shop. Bolan walked cautiously up the ramp, his hand on the grip of the Desert Eagle under his T-shirt.

Halfway up, he stopped. Through large picture windows he could see men and women sitting around the informal dining room. Wearing a casual mixture of beachwear and scuba gear, they laughed uproariously as one of the men finished a story.

He scanned the room. The only phone was mounted against the wall, well within earshot.

The hotel's guests knew nothing of the cartel's presence on the island, but he didn't need them overhearing his phone call and passing on information if the Peruvians showed up later.

Bolan retraced his steps down the ramp and continued along the beach, passing the oil tanks he'd seen from the highway, then another set of cottages. A few minutes later the Seaview Hotel appeared out of the darkness.

Two stories high, the main building consisted of an open bar facing the beach and a dining room visible through the windows. Guest rooms ran the length of the second floor.

The Executioner paused, scanning the second-story doors. High ground would be an advantage if Mariategui located them, but he couldn't risk the lives of innocents in the other rooms. He glanced back at the cottages. Several, including the one farthest from the bar, were dark.

The warrior checked to make sure the Desert Eagle was hidden under his shirt, then crossed the beach to the office at the front of the building.

A young man looked up as he entered the office. He wore a short-sleeved safari shirt, unbuttoned to the waist. At least a dozen gold chains, black coral ornaments dangling from most, hung across his hairless chest.

"Need a room, man?" he asked as Bolan crossed the threshold.

"Cottage, if you've got it. Last one on the far end would be nice."

Bolan saw his eyes fly from the straw hat to the Sir Turtle T-shirt, then drop to the Executioner's soiled jeans and shoes.

The warrior watched the kid draw his own conclusions. He knew he didn't look as if he'd just stepped off the plane from Miami. He'd obviously been here long enough to buy a stupid hat, a T-shirt and get dirty.

Which meant he had another room somewhere on the island. A room that probably had a wife waiting in it.

Fine. Let the kid think what he wanted. The Executioner could use the situation to his advantage.

The young man winked. "Ah, man. Got just what you need." He turned toward the keyboard on the wall behind him. "Privacy, yeah? Cottage nine." He turned back to Bolan, set the key on the counter and winked. "Variety be the spice of life, right? Little new stuff never hurt." Pulling a registration card from a drawer behind the counter, he dropped it next to the key.

Bolan took the key. Ignoring the card, he placed several rumpled bills on the counter.

The young man looked down. "Too much."

The Executioner shook his head. "I'm going to make a phone call. And there's a little extra for you. I'm not here, and never was. You understand?"

A shrewd, knowing, man-of-the-world smile stretched across the kid's features. He dropped the registration card back in the drawer. "Have a good night, Mr. Smith from New York City."

Bolan hurried back along the beach to the cottage. Inside he switched on the light and closed the door behind him. The phone sat on a splintery wooden table between two twin beds. The Executioner lifted his wrist, checking the time. It was well after closing time at Justice, but he knew Brognola would be there.

Lifting the receiver, Bolan dialed the Justice man's office direct. He studied the heavy oak ceiling beams over his head as he waited for the line to connect.

Brognola answered before the first ring finished. "Hello?"

"Me, Hal. I'm on an unsecured line, and we don't have much time. I've lost contact with my flyboy—"

"Hang on, friend," the big Fed interrupted. "You've been out of pocket. Let me fill you in from this end."

"Shoot."

"Ace called in, maybe an hour ago. He's been staying out of sight. The law got him confused with the unfriendlies. Try South West Point."

Bolan pulled the map from his pocket. "Got ya. The cargo and I are about halfway in between. If Ace's safe, I'd just as soon leave him."

"He's safe."

"A mutual friend needs medical attention quick." The Executioner paused and took a deep breath. "I know what the Cayman bureaucrats said about intervention, Hal, but this place is crawling with hostiles."

"No problem. They're begging for help now. To make a long story short, three planeloads of Recon Arrest Teams took off from Miami fifteen minutes ago."

Bolan felt a hard smile cross his face. Recon Arrest Teams. RATS—small attack units made up of Special Forces soldiers led by DEA agents trained in combat. That should do the trick.

If they got there in time.

As if reading his mind, Brognola continued. "They'll touch down at Owens Roberts airport in another half hour. Then, however long it takes them across land. Where will you be?"

Bolan paused. Reuben wouldn't last much longer on the shore. He needed someplace to rest. And whatever emergency medical attention the Executioner could provide. "The Seaview Hotel, Hal," he said. "Cottage nine." He gave the Justice man directions.

"Fine. I'll get word to the RATS before they land." Brognola paused, then said, "Be careful, Striker."

"There's no other way. Just hope nobody's listening in." Bolan hung up.

He closed the cottage door, pocketed the key and took off along the beach once more, jogging through the sand and over the iron shore.

As he passed the Casa Bertmar, two gunshots rang out from the direction of Smith Cove.

"What the hell was that?" a voice from the dining room asked loudly.

"Ah, shit," another voice slurred. "Car backfiring's all."

Bolan broke into a sprint, his legs churning, sand flying beneath his feet. As he neared the cove, four more pierced the silence.

Pistol shots. The Beretta he'd left with Tana? Reuben's SIG?

He strained for speed, his lungs threatening to burst as he flew across the beach.

REUBEN NEEDS YOU. Reuben needs you. Reuben needs you. Tana felt her lips move silently as she mouthed the words. She glanced toward her husband, lying as still as death in the shallow cavity beneath the rock overhang. She forced her eyes toward the ocean. A second later they flew back to Reuben, and she strained through the darkness to watch his chest move up and down.

Tana shifted slightly, and the gun at her side bit into her thigh. She shifted again, then looked down at the weapon Belasko had given her—practically forced on her. It was big and black, *ugly*.

Her hand shaking, she reached gingerly toward the gun. Her fingertips traced along the smooth steel, damp with ocean spray. Her index finger brushed the trigger.

Tana's hand jerked back as if she'd touched a hot stove.

Could she kill someone, take a life? She didn't know.

She checked Reuben's breathing again, then forced her eyes back to the gun. Slowly she reached for it, forcing herself to pick it up. Grasping it with both hands, she kept her fingers far away from the trigger. She held it in front of her. It was heavy.

Gently, afraid it might detonate with her every movement, Tana lowered the gun to the rocks behind her where she wouldn't have to see it.

The frightened woman leaned toward her husband, pressing an index finger against his wrist. His pulse was slow but regular. Maybe he was just exhausted. She placed the wrist over his chest, and a chill ran down her spine. Reuben looked like a corpse.

Tana moved his arm to his side.

"Oh, please, honey," she whispered. A salty tear rolled into her mouth as she formed the words. "*Please* wake up and help me."

Miraculously the lids rolled back over Reuben's eyes. He stared sightlessly upward at the rock above his head. Tana took his hand in both of hers, squeezed tightly and rested her head on his shoulder.

She felt Reuben's other hand cover hers and sat back, staring deep into his muddled eyes. Somewhere in that oblivious gaze, she saw a flicker of recognition. Then Reuben's lips moved slowly, awkwardly. "Be . . . all right," he mumbled.

Suddenly the tiny cave lit up with the illumination of a thousand candles. Tana turned toward the light, the beam blinding her.

Then the light shifted, hitting Reuben full in the face. He stared ahead, unblinking.

"Boss!" a voice called out from behind the light. "Over here!"

Through constricted pupils, Tana saw the blurry form of a man. He moved the front part of his shotgun back and forth along the barrel, and the sound of metal against metal echoed into the rock cavity.

Radio static blared and a voice said, "Don't kill them. I'm coming."

As her eyes began to dilate once more, Tana saw that the man wore the same type of multicolored army clothing Belasko had worn in the jungle. Just behind him, to his left, a similarly dressed man held a handgun in one hand and a walkie-talkie in the other. Her vision cleared further, and Tana saw white teeth flash in the darkness as both men smiled diabolically.

"We'll be rewarded," the man with the walkie-talkie whispered to his partner.

Tana felt a quick movement to her side. As she turned, two explosions echoed within the rock depression, threatening to deafen her. Bright red-and-yellow flames shot out in the darkness next to her, and for a brief instant she thought Reuben had somehow started a fire.

The men before her dropped to the ground. Tana saw Reuben's gun in his hand, her husband staring apathetically ahead into the darkness.

Then, as if the weight of the gun had suddenly become more than Reuben could bear, it fell from his fingers to the ground.

He lay back slowly and closed his eyes.

Running footsteps came from the rocks overhead. Tana leaned over her husband, shaking his shoulders frantically. "Reuben," she whispered. "Reuben?"

No response.

"Reuben?" Tana said louder as the footsteps neared, then screamed, "Reuben!"

A dark form dropped the short distance from the rock overhang to the iron shore in front of her. Turning quickly, Tana saw the reflection of a huge silver gun in the man's hands. Then a white scar gleamed in the moonlight.

She closed her eyes, trying to force this vision of Satan from her brain.

Mariategui trained his gun on Reuben's prostrate body. "It is good to see you, Cha-cha." Tana recognized the voice. "I had hoped to find you earlier. Have you had a pleasant stay in the Caymans?" Mariategui paused, waiting for an answer. "Cha-cha?"

"He's unconcious," Tana whispered.

Mariategui moved cautiously forward and knelt. His eyes fell to Reuben's gun on the ground. He stuck it into his waistband, then shook the DEA man roughly. Getting no response, he spit in Reuben's face and returned to his feet.

"Cha-cha," Mariategui said, shaking his head. "It's a pity. I'd prepared quite a speech for you before I killed you."

Tana stared up to the hard face and saw no pity, no mercy in the eyes flashing with hatred, none of the kindness or gentility Reuben had spoken of.

Then a flicker of a smile curled Mariategui's lips before his faced beamed in delight. "Ah." He turned from Reuben to Tana. "Rather than waste my efforts, perhaps *you* will hear what I have to say...before I kill you both." He paused, then threw back his head and laughed.

Mariategui stooped to the ground, retrieved the fallen flashlight and wedged it within a sharp formation of rock, the beam angling toward him. "We'll do it right, Mrs. Gonzales. And then you'll both die for your husband's treachery."

He shoved the silver gun into his waistband next to Reuben's weapon and stepped into the spot from the flashlight.

Tana saw him squint for a moment and remembered the strength of the beam in her own eyes.

Grinning down at her, Mariategui said, "How do I look, Mrs. Gonzalez?"

She felt her mind trying to slip away, trying to deny the reality of the situation, retreat from this sudden climax to the nightmare she had lived with for the past two days. She forced herself to turn toward her husband, sleeping peacefully, unknowingly, at her side.

"We were like brothers, your husband and I," Mariategui began. "We hunted together, fished in the streams of..."

Tana concentrated, trying to will her hand to move. Her arm felt as if it weighed a thousand pounds.

"Your husband was accepted into my home," Mariategui continued. "He ate at my table...."

Slowly, sluggishly, Tana's hand moved behind her back. Her fingers brushed the cold, slick metal.

"When my wife gave birth, Cha-cha was there. He was the godfather to my son...."

She lifted the weapon, willed her arm to swing rapidly around. Like a slow-motion rerun, or a dream in which she couldn't force herself to speed up, Tana saw the gun appear in front of her.

Pull the trigger, her brain screamed, hard the first time. The second time will be easier....

"We spoke of the day when we would run the cartel ourselves...." she heard Mariategui say as if from somewhere far away. "We'd divide Hector Pizarro's responsibilities between us, each having an equal say in matters, as we expanded the cartel to cover the entire..."

Pull the trigger. Pull the trigger.

No. He's a human being. Life is sacred. *Sacred*. Thou shall not kill.

"We would trust each other, your husband and I, never fearing that one was maneuvering to take control...."

Mariategui's voice suddenly rose an octave. "But he betrayed that trust!" he screamed behind the flashlight. "And now he'll die!"

Tana watched as the screaming man drew the silver gun and pointed it at her helpless husband.

Reuben needs you!

She heard the explosion, felt the gun jump in her hand. Flame shot from the barrel as it had from Reuben's gun, and before she knew what was happening, the gun jumped again, then again.

Then again.

11

Bolan raced past Smith Cove and leapt up onto the ragged outcropping of rocks. Jumping from formation to formation, he unholstered the Desert Eagle as he raced toward Reuben and Tana.

As he neared, the warrior saw the outlines of three bodies lying in front of the small cove. Two of the men wore cammies, the third, a white silk suit.

Marino Mariategui. The Lima cartel underboss had fallen to his side. The beam of a flashlight propped in the rocks shone brightly on his face.

His open eyes stared vacantly into the light. A tiny trail of blood trickled from the corner of his mouth, following the scar line down his cheek to fall in an ever-widening pool on the rock beneath his chin.

Tana sat exactly where he'd left her, her knees tucked under her chin, arms locked tightly around her ankles. The woman looked even smaller than before.

The Beretta 93-R lay at her feet, and she stared aimlessly out at the ocean. Bolan knelt at her side, discerning what had transpired in a heartbeat.

In spite of her limitations, Tana Gonzalez had come through.

"Are you okay?" he asked.

Tana stared into his eyes. "I . . . killed him," she stammered.

"Good. Now, let's get on with it." He shoved the Desert Eagle back in his belt and hauled her to her feet. "We've got to get Reuben out of here, Tana. It's not over yet."

The Executioner heard movement down the beach, and the Desert Eagle jumped back into his hand. Then a familiar voice whispered through the darkness. "Striker?"

Jack Grimaldi stepped from the shadows.

Bolan scanned the area as the pilot jogged toward them. They were still clear, but they had only minutes, maybe seconds before the whole area swarmed with cartel gunners. If he and Grimaldi had heard shots, the Peruvians would have, too.

The Executioner glanced to the walkie-talkies on the ground. There was a damn good chance Mariategui had radioed his position to the others around the island, as well.

"We've got to get out of here, Jack. I've rented a cottage up the beach. Seaview Hotel, Number nine, in case we get separated again." He pointed toward the scattered weapons. "Give me a hand with the guns. We'll need all the firepower we can round up."

Bolan leaned down, grabbing a Winchester riot gun next to one of the dead men. He found Reuben's SIG-Sauer in Mariategui's waistband and slid it into his jeans next to the Beretta. He saw Grimaldi stuff two M-16 magazines into his back pocket, then pry the assault rifle from the fingers of the other cartel hitter.

The ace pilot lifted a nickel-plated Government Model 9 mm pistol from the ground near Mariategui.

Bolan found a Beretta 92-F—the civilian model of his 93-R—in a hip holster on one of the bodies, which he extended toward Tana. "Works the same as the other one."

The woman hesitated, then nodded and took the weapon, letting it hang loosely at the end of her arm.

Bolan lifted the walkie-talkie from the ground. Switching it back on, he heard an unknown voice in Spanish.

"Yes, yes! The boss has cornered them near the place known as Smith Cove. We're almost there."

"Let's go," Bolan said. He slung the shotgun over his shoulder and lifted Reuben to his back.

They took off at a jog across the craggy shore, then sped up when they hit flatter land. He carried the Desert Eagle in his right hand, holding the DEA agent's arms tightly around his neck with the other.

Overhead, Bolan heard planes. He looked up and saw the lights of three aircraft dip their wings and turn back toward the airport on the other side of George Town.

"C-130 transports," the pilot stated. "The cavalry's just arrived."

"Not yet," Bolan answered, "but they're close. We've got to hold out somehow until they find us. If we can get to the cottage without being spotted—"

Suddenly shots rang out from behind. Bolan glanced over his shoulder to see the red-and-yellow flames of muzzle blasts and the dark, shadowy forms of a dozen men racing after them.

He twisted as he ran, snapping off two .44 Magnums. The cartel man in the lead hit the sand face-first.

Grimaldi paused, firing a long burst from the M-16, then sprinted back to catch up to Bolan and Tana.

"Should I shoot?" Tana asked, winded.

"Just run," Bolan ordered.

More rounds splattered into the wet sand around their feet. Each volley came closer as the cartel gunners adjusted their arms. Bolan stopped, turned again and fired four times, each round scoring a hit.

Grimaldi laid down support fire with the M-16, sending a steady stream of rounds through the group and downing two more.

The remaining hitters slowed their pace.

Bolan, Grimaldi and Tana sprinted on along the shore, passing the Casa Bertmar. The Executioner glanced up to see several curious tourists coming down the ramp to investigate the commotion.

He turned again, fired a quick round toward the pursuers, then kept going. The massive Magnum had been fired for the benefit of the patrons of Casa Bertmar. It had a message attached to it—get back from the beach.

The people on the ramp caught on, scrambling over one another up the ramp to disappear inside the dining room.

They passed the oil tanks, and the Executioner saw the cottage in the distance. Ten feet from the door, he stopped abruptly and fired three more times at the oncoming cartel men.

The Peruvians dived to the ground as the slide of the Desert Eagle locked open, empty.

Bolan jumped the weapon back in his jeans and drew the Beretta as he ran for the door. Ten feet away he lowered a shoulder, struck the wood and burst into the cottage.

Tana followed. Grimaldi paused at the door, firing another burst of .223s at their pursuers before ducking through the opening and slamming the door behind him.

Bolan dropped Reuben on one of the beds and turned to Grimaldi. "Get them into the bathroom."

Without a word the Stony Man pilot lifted the DEA agent and carried him through the door, Tana at his heels.

Bolan raced to the window, peering through the wooden slats of the venetian blinds. Scattered along the beach, he saw the dark forms of the remaining men—seven or eight—cautiously approaching the cottage. He drew the Desert Eagle, rammed a fresh magazine up the grip, then stuck it back in his belt as Grimaldi came back out of the bathroom.

The pilot joined him on the other side of the window. Grimaldi dropped the M-16 magazine from his weapon, checked the load, then replaced it with a full one from his back pocket.

Both men turned as the roar of engines sounded at the front of the cottage. Bolan moved to the opposite window and saw a dozen vehicles arrive. Fresh troops poured out of the cars and took up positions behind trees, trash receptacles and other available cover.

"Cover the back," the Executioner instructed Grimaldi. "I'll take the front." He unslung the Winchester and pumped the slide, throwing a shell onto the floor. Slugs. Good.

Bolan knelt, retrieved the slug and jammed it back into the magazine. Leaning forward, he separated the blinds with the Winchester's barrel. He sighted along the length of the weapon, dropping the shotgun's bead sight on the chest of a hardguy half-hidden behind a trash can.

"You ready, Jack?"

"Let the games begin," the Stony Man pilot replied.

Bolan pulled the trigger. The deer slug burst through the glass and then shredded the chest of the gunner behind the trash can. As he fell from cover, the Executioner worked the slide, then turned the pump gun on a man next to a tall palm tree. He drove another round through the window and into the man's face, the huge lead bullet nearly decapitating the corpse.

The warrior dropped beneath the window.

A second later the cartel hitters cut loose with their M-16s. Hundreds of rounds flew through the windows, front and back, drilling into the walls and the overhead beams. Razor-edged shards of glass exploded over Bolan's and Grimaldi's heads. The venetian blinds shredded into thousands of finger-length splinters, sailing through the air as dust and scraps of plaster rained down from the walls.

Bolan pumped the shotgun again and stood. He tapped the trigger, and a gunman in cammies charging the door went down, another of the deadly slugs hammering through his chest to leave an inch-wide hole.

Bolan jumped again, fired, pumped, fired, another cartel killer dropping under each slug.

Behind him, the Executioner heard the steady purr of the M-16 as Grimaldi held the trigger back against the guard.

Dropping the empty riot gun, the warrior drew the Desert Eagle from his waistband. Seven .44 Magnums flamed from the barrel, seven cartel hitters fell to the earth.

"How's it look on your end?" the Executioner yelled over the clamor.

"Still coming!" Grimaldi yelled as the M-16 rattled dry in his hands. The Stony Man pilot let it fall from his grip and drew the nickel-plated Government Model Colt. "And I'm out of mags, Sarge."

Bolan turned back to the window, looking down at the open slide of the Desert Eagle.

So was he.

The Executioner drew the Beretta and thumbed the selector to 3-round burst. Flipping the front grip down from beneath the barrel, he held the 93-R in both hands and sent three rounds screeching out the window and into the throat of another charging Peruvian. He dropped beneath the window again as another barrage sailed through the shapeless crater.

Suddenly the gunfire ceased outside.

The Executioner rose slightly, peering over the edge of the ragged wall. Behind the parked cars a dozen more vehicles came to a halt.

At least forty more cartel gunmen leapt from the vehicles, entering the field of play.

Bolan dropped back to the floor, his back to the wall. He took a deep breath, then checked his remaining ammo. The Beretta's magazine, his last, still held twelve rounds. He dropped the clip from Reuben's SIG. Six.

Both the shotgun and Desert Eagle lay useless at his feet.

"How you fixed, Jack?" he called across the room.

Grimaldi looked over his shoulder. The ace pilot shook his head. He shook the shiny pistol in his hand. "Two rounds left in this pimp gun," he said. "I still got a full wheel in my Smith. Besides that..." Grimaldi's voice trailed off.

"Pick your shots. Each one's got to count."

The pilot nodded.

Bolan turned back to the window as the most ferocious assault yet drilled through the walls. Large, gaping holes appeared in the wallboard between the wooden two-by-four studs. Behind him the Executioner heard a crash, then a grunt.

He turned to see Grimaldi pinned under a pile of thick oak ceiling beams.

Bolan started toward him, then another barrage of gunfire drove him back to the floor. "Jack!" he shouted. "Can you hear me?"

No answer.

The Executioner felt the anger surge through him. He rose again, firing through a hole in the wall and dropping a man next to the cars.

A round nicked his arm from behind, and the Executioner twisted, snapping a slug into the face of a man standing in the rear window. The man fell forward, half in, half out of the demolished cottage.

Bolan crawled across the floor through the waste as more rounds sailed over his head. Grimaldi lay, eyes closed, on the bullet-shredded carpet, blood pouring from his scalp.

The Executioner parted his friend's hair, finding the contusion where one of the beams had struck the pilot. Dropping the Beretta at his side, he reached down and grasped the beam. The Executioner groaned, the muscles in his arms and shoulders straining, threatening to snap as he tried to pry the heavy lumber from the man.

The beams shifted slightly, then settled back in place.

"Jack! Can you hear me?"

Still no response.

The firing outside ceased once more.

Bolan lifted the Beretta and scooted back against the wall next to the pilot. He stared straight ahead, taking in both windows with his peripheral vision.

He knew what was happening. By now the Peruvians had figured out that the men in the cottage were low on ammunition. They'd be talking, planning, getting ready for their final assault.

Bolan switched the Beretta to semiauto and yanked Reuben's SIG-Sauer from his jeans. Flipping the safety, he held the SIG in his left hand, the Beretta in his right.

He waited for what he knew was inevitable, reminding himself that this day was long overdue.

Gunfire rang out but no rounds were aimed at the cottage. The Executioner frowned. He rose to his knees and crawled to the opening.

The hitters had moved from behind their cars. They faced away from him, toward the road. Past the parked vehicles the Executioner saw two dozen Cayman Island police cars come tearing down the highway and screech to a halt. Men—Americans—streamed from the vehicles.

Some of the men carried Colt 9 mm carbines and wore blue nylon windbreakers. Others carried M-16s and wore tiger-striped camouflaged fatigues.

All of the RATS, regardless of what they wore or carried, sent steady streams of automatic fire into the teams of killers from Peru.

It was over in minutes.

Bolan turned toward the mass of ceiling beams on the floor. Beneath the lumber Grimaldi's eyes had opened.

"You okay?" the warrior asked.

"Got a bitch of a headache, Striker. How about getting me out of here?"

The bathroom door cracked open, and Tana's face appeared in the opening. "Can we come out now?"

Bolan smiled at her. "I don't see why not."

EPILOGUE

The Executioner glanced at his watch. By now, Reuben and Tana Gonzalez would be touching down in Washington. It had been touch and go at the George Town hospital for a few hours, and Reuben would still be confined to a D.C. hospital for several days to undergo observation. But the scrappy little DEA agent looked as if he'd be ready to testify long before the slow arm of the law got around to trying his cases.

Bolan's mind returned to what Reuben had said about Hector Pizarro. "I blew it, Belasko. The big fish got away."

The warrior slowed his vehicle as he reached the Lima city limits. Grimaldi had needed only a few stitches. The hard-headed Stony Man pilot had been more than up to flying him to Peru.

He stopped at a streetlight, waiting. He watched as several couples dressed in evening wear crossed in front of him toward a nightclub across the street. They laughed as they jostled each other for position under their umbrellas.

When the light changed, he pulled forward another two blocks, then cut down a side street, parking the nondescript rental car under a streetlight in front of the Pizarro building. He glanced up to the top of the building as he crossed the street.

Several lights burned in the revolving penthouse.

Bolan pushed through the glass door and strode purposely to the guard station in the lobby. Behind the desk a bored man in the uniform of a rent-a-cop sat with his feet on the desk, his eyes glued to a skin magazine.

He glanced up in time to take the Executioner's right cross squarely on the jaw.

Bolan bound the man's hands behind him with a plastic strip-cuff. He stuffed a gag in his mouth, then lowered the man out of sight behind the desk. He took the elevator to the top floor, stepped off and silently climbed the stairs to the penthouse. Pulling a pick set from the pocket of his coat, he went to work on the door. Seconds later he heard the tumblers roll, and the door snapped open.

Bolan moved through the door, quietly closing it behind him. In the center of the outer office stood a large oak desk, the top clear except for a leather-cased manicure set and a bottle of nail polish.

A bright yellow blouse hung from the back of the desk chair.

The warrior lifted the blouse from the chair as he approached a closed door in the far wall. Pressing his ear against the wood, he heard soft, feminine giggles on the other side. He stepped back, drawing the suppressed Beretta from beneath his coat. Lifting his right foot to knee level, he kicked out, and the door swung inward.

A tall, topless woman stood in the middle of the elaborate office, unbuckling Hector Pizarro's belt. She looked up in surprise as Bolan stepped into the room, the Beretta in one hand, her blouse in the other. Dropping Pizarro's belt, she threw her hands in the air.

The cartel godfather's slacks slid to his ankles.

Bolan threw the woman's blouse across the room to her. "Get dressed, and get out."

She snatched her blouse out of the air and headed for the door.

Hector Pizarro looked stupidly down at his feet, his face coloring with humiliation. He started to reach for his pants, but Bolan fired a round an inch past his legs, and the chubby hands jerked high over his head.

The man froze in fear. "You're the American who helped Gonzalez."

Bolan nodded.

Pizarro returned the nod, then his face relaxed. He hooked a thumb over his shoulders, and Bolan saw several dozen piranhas swimming back and forth across an aquarium. "We're both piranha, you and I. We take what we want. But like the fish in the tank, we can exist together."

"Can we?"

Pizarro smiled. "Of course. Now, I don't wish to waste my time bartering. Name your price. You shall have it."

Bolan stared at him, the Beretta aimed at a spot halfway between his eyes.

Pizarro shook his head. "Hurry. I'm getting tired of asking you. How much do you want?"

The Executioner continued to stare at the fat man. He'd been asked that question many times over the years. He was tired of it, too. So tired, he decided to remain silent.

The Beretta 93-R answered for him, a 9 mm hollowpoint coring the drug czar's flabby face.

Bolan reholstered the Beretta as he descended the stairs. He pushed the elevator button and waited as the car creaked to a halt at the top of the shaft. When the door opened, he stepped in.

There'd always be fish who got away in a system that allowed for loopholes in the law. But Hector Pizarro wouldn't be one of them.

Go for a hair-raising ride in

JAMES AXLER

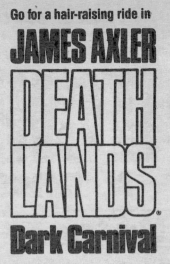

DEATH LANDS

Dark Carnival

Trapped in an evil baron's playground, the rides are downhill and dangerous for Ryan Cawdor and his roving band of warrior-survivalists.

For one brief moment after their narrow escape, Ryan thinks they have found the peace and idyll they so desperately seek. But a dying messenger delivers a dark message....